SAM WHITTAKER

I BOUGHT A HAUNTED SCHOOL

Copyright © 2024 by Sam Whittaker

All rights reserved.

Cover Design: Miblart

No portion of this book may be reproduced in any form without written permission from the publisher or author, except as permitted by U.S. copyright law.

Contents

A Change of Fortune?	1
1. Ava	3
2. Floppy	9
3. Mommy	16
4. Visitor	22
5. Crash	30
6. Bed	39
7. Intruder	46
8. Dog	51
Two Dead at Old School	57
9. Setup	59
10. Explore	65
11. Boy	73
Student Missing	78
12. Somnambulism	80
13. Search	86

14. Shopping	93
15. Malfunction	99
16. Shadow	107
School Suspended Following Tragedy	112
17. Patrick	113
18. Joe	119
19. Revenge	125
20. Guests	134
21. Dinner	141
22. Trap	148
23. Studio	156
24. Window	162
25. Web	168
School Closes Indefinitely	178
Epilogue	180
Trial Conclusion	184

A Change of Fortune?

The following is a selection of an article from the Cedar Park Herald, a local newspaper. Dated: July 19, 2024

Who says you can't have a new lease on life? It appears that one can... even if one is an old, abandoned school building.

The facility that once housed Cedar Park School has been purchased at auction. Rumors have it that the old school will be both home to a family as well as a recording studio.

Long-time residents will of course be familiar with the sordid history of the building and the past tragedies associated with it. Even new generations are known to whisper legends about the place as they scurry past it on their way to somewhere else.

The empty building has long been a point of contention with township officials. It has previously been sold more than once, only to have the deal fall through or flatly refused before possession is transferred.

Perhaps these new arrivals can breathe new life into the tired structure of the storied building.

1

Ava

Ava trembled as she hid in the bushes across the street. Alternating blue and red lights splashed across her face in the darkness as she watched the strange happenings before her. She had been hiding like this for about half an hour.

There was a flurry of activity outside of what was supposed to have been her new home. She was six years old and not used to the idea of being by herself like this in the dark. She didn't like it.

The police moved about the scene and traveled in groups. One or two were by themselves. She saw some of them inside, passing in front of the windows. She worried for them.

Her Mommy and Daddy had bought the strange old building that had once been a school and intended to convert it into a livable space as well as a place for them to work. They had raved about the idea. Well, at least Mommy had. Daddy seemed a little skeptical about the whole project.

She saw a shadowed figure a few paces ahead stop and turn her way. The head tilted to one side. Ava hunched lower into the bushes, hugging the ragged stuffed rabbit closely to her chest.

The silhouetted person headed her way. She fought the urge to break away and run.

When the person arrived, they crouched low and, in a kind, feminine voice said, "Hello? Is someone there?"

She kept still and quiet.

"I'm a Detective with the police department," came the soothing voice. "I'm here to help. Can you come out, please?"

She remained frozen in place, not wanting to give herself away.

A hand reached forward and pulled aside several of the branches of the bush behind which Ava hid. Before she knew it, she was staring into the comforting face of a middle-aged black woman.

"Hello," the woman said. "My name is Detective Byrd. What's yours?"

Ava simply stared at the woman with terrified eyes. She didn't move, save to clutch the ratty old rabbit closer to her.

"You don't want to talk? That's okay." The woman paused, considered something, then tried a different approach. She turned to face the building on the opposite side of the street. "Do you live here?" the woman asked in a casual tone, nodding toward the old school building. She looked back at Ava.

Ava said nothing

"You have blood on you," Detective Byrd observed. "Are you hurt, sweetheart?"

Ava shook her head violently from side to side, but tears formed in her eyes and spilled freely down her cheeks.

"You do live here, don't you?" the woman said. "We are here to help. Would you please come with me?"

Ava shook her head again.

"It would be better if you do," Byrd said. "It's not safe for a little girl to stay out here like this when there's no one to watch after you."

Now Ava broke down into a full sob. She crumpled, squeezing the stuffed rabbit.

The woman stood and motioned for somebody to come over. But Ava was too busy crying to care.

"Excuse me, officer," she said to the man who just appeared. "Will you help me, please? I think we found a survivor."

The officer turned his face and observed Ava for the first time. Surprise covered his countenance. He muttered a curse under his breath.

He leaned over to the Detective and said, "What do you want me to do?"

Detective Byrd half turned her face to him and said barely loud enough for Ava to hear, "If she runs, I need you to catch her for me."

Then the woman came through the bushes and crouched beside Ava's fallen form. She reached down to pick her up. That's when Ava bolted into action. She was on her feet in no time, scrambling to get away. But the officer was fast. He had blocked her path and crouched down quick as lightning and hugged his arms around her to prevent her from getting away.

Ava thrashed and screamed. "No," she shrieked. "No, let me go!"

"Easy, honey," the officer said, gritting his teeth as he struggled to keep hold of her writhing form. "We're just trying to help. Calm down!"

"Mommy and Daddy!" she wailed. "I want my Mommy and Daddy."

"I know," Detective Byrd said, coming up to her and resting both hands on her shoulders to still her. "I know," she repeated quieter. There was a look of sorrow on the woman's face.

Ava understood the look. Ava would not be seeing her Mommy and Daddy again. Nor any of the others. Not that never seeing the others bothered her.

"Have you ever ridden in a police car?" Detective Byrd asked.

Ava melted into the other officer's arms, boneless. She whimpered but gave no other reply.

"I can take you to a special place," Detective Byrd said. "Far away from here where you don't have to worry. How does that sound?"

"I want my Mommy and Daddy," Ava replied.

"Put her in the passenger front seat of my car," Byrd said to the officer. "I need to take her downtown."

***

Ava sat, hugging her ratty old rabbit doll to her chest in a small room with a table, four chairs, and a giant mirror on one wall. Her shoulders were hunched forward, and her face was buried in the back of the rabbit's head. The occasional tear sprung to her eyes and cascaded down her dirty cheeks, but the worst of the sobbing seemed to be behind her.

It had been what felt like forever since Detective Byrd had been in the room with her. Ava was by herself now. But she felt like she was being watched. She knew she was.

The door opened and Detective Byrd came in, carrying a steaming cup.

She closed the door behind her and maneuvered herself to the opposite side of the table. She set the cup in front of Ava and said, "Do you like hot chocolate?"

Ava looked at the steaming cup and then flicked her eyes to the detective. Her focus returned to the hot chocolate, and she tentatively reached for the cup. She took it and slowly pulled it back to herself. She lifted the steaming cup to her face and took a long sniff.

It smelled good. She put the cup to her lips and taste-tested it. It was very hot. She jerked her lips away and set the cup back down on the table.

"Maybe we better let it cool down first," Detective Byrd said. Ava gave a small nod of acknowledgment and looked away.

There was a long pause then Detective Byrd said, "Ava? Can you tell me what happened tonight?"

The little girl's worried eyes shot to the detective. Her lip quivered and fresh tears sprang unbidden to her eyes.

"Bad things," she said. "Bad people."

"Was it a robbery?" the detective asked. "Did people come wanting something? Something that your mom and dad had?"

Ava stopped and thought about this. It wasn't right. She shook her head slowly.

"Do you know who they were?" the detective asked.

"A mean boy," Ava repeated in a hushed tone.

"Have you seen him before?" the detective asked.

Ava nodded.

"When?" Byrd asked.

"After we moved in," Ava replied.

"Do you know if he lives around here? Is he from your street?"

Ava shook her head slowly. "He doesn't live anywhere."

"Do you mean he is homeless?" Detective Byrd asked.

Ava slowly shook her head once more.

"No," Ava said. "He doesn't *live*."

"What do you mean honey?" Byrd said, narrowing her eyes.

Clutching the rabbit all the tighter to her chest, Ava leaned forward and said, "He died a long time ago."

2

Floppy

It was move-in day.

An army of movers bustled about carrying furniture and large boxes into the old school building and came out empty-handed once again. Ava stood with her Daddy. He directed a few of the movers to bring their current burdens to a particular room on the second floor. Her Mommy was nowhere in sight.

"Daddy?" Ava said.

"Hold on sweetie," the man replied. He was in the middle of a conversation with three movers bearing large crates. "That's sensitive sound equipment," he said. "Some of it is quite expensive. And the microphones can be a bit finicky and fragile. So please, when you set them down make sure not to pack any other boxes on top of them. Got that?"

The three gruff men holding the crates grunted but otherwise seemed uninterested in paying attention to what the man said. They knew their business, and they understood what 'fragile' scrawled on the sides of the boxes meant.

One of them managed to say, "Yes sir." The three of them shared looks, then moved on.

"Daddy?" Ava said, a little more insistent.

"What is it, sweetheart?" her father replied, sounding a touch impatient.

"You said I could get a new dolly," Ava said.

"I said you could get a dolly *after* we moved in," Daddy replied, his patience now not much more than a thin veneer. "We still have a few hours of work left. It will probably have to wait until tomorrow. We'll go out shopping and you can remind us then. We will get you a dolly then. Okay?"

"Daddy, how am I supposed to sleep without a new dolly?"

"You slept plenty of nights without the new dolly before," Daddy pointed out. "Why should now be any different?"

Ava stared up at the old school building, a nervous twitch tugged at one cheek.

"Because," she said, "I don't know this place." She leaned toward him conspiratorially and added, "It scares me."

He couldn't hide the smirk that appeared in response to his child's innocent confession. "There is no reason to be scared," Daddy said. "It's just different. It's not bad."

"I don't like it, Daddy," she said.

"It's going to be fine, baby," he said. "It will just take some getting used to, that's all. Besides, look – your Mommy and I have been working on this for years. And your Mommy is really excited about the opportunities this affords her. Can you try to be a least a little happy for her?"

"I am," she said not sounding happy at all. "It's just…" She trailed off as she cast another glance in the direction of the school-turned-home.

"I know," he said. "It's a very different kind of place than we've ever lived in but trust me; this is going to be great. You got all kinds of space to run around and play in here."

"It's so big," she said. "Won't I get lost?"

He threw his head back and laughed. "It's not that big," he said. "It's way smaller than any school I ever went to. It just *looks* big because it's got two floors and two wings."

The old school hadn't been open for over thirty years. It was L-shaped containing eight classrooms on the top floor. Each wing of the upper floor had four classrooms. The bottom floor had classrooms, an office, and a cafeteria. There was also a lobby area connected to the cafeteria right when one walked into the building.

"I've got an idea," Daddy said. "Why don't you go inside and find Mommy? She should be upstairs."

"Go inside?" Ava said. "By myself?"

"You won't be by yourself," he said. "There's all kinds of people here. And as I said, Mommy is inside. I'm sure she'd love to see you."

She hugged her arms around her middle and a shiver ran through her as she stared at the old school building. "Are we really going to live here, Daddy?" she asked.

He chuckled and shook his head. "You bet we are, sweetheart. And it will be fantastic. You'll see. It will just take a little getting used to, is all."

"Are you sure, Daddy?" she asked.

"I am positive," he answered. Even at six years old, she detected the doubt in his voice. She knew that Mommy was the one who wanted to buy the old school. She wanted to set up recording studios and offices for her special work. Daddy always helped her with her business, and he was good at it. But sometimes she got the impression that her Daddy and herself were just along for the ride when it came to Mommy's music and recording.

"Run along now," he said.

She looked up at him one last time and nodded. She stared back at the school for several long heartbeats then took her first step. Then came the next, which was easier. And then the rest. She burst into a sudden run as she rushed toward the entrance of the building.

Ava almost ran into the legs of a mover coming out the door. She skidded to a halt just in time.

"Whoa there, little lady," he said. "Don't want to get trampled." He turned his vast body to the side and stepped back, allowing her space to come through.

She looked up at him solemnly, nodded, and then rushed through the door.

She was standing in the vast cafeteria space, or at least it seemed vast to her. At most, it would have accommodated thirty students on its best day.

Once inside, Ava meandered and dodged around the legs of movers and stacks of boxes. She ran to the opposite side of the cafeteria and through the set of double doors. She found herself in a long hallway. She coursed through, continuing to navigate the stacks of boxes, furniture, and the lumbering form of the occasional mover. She reached the end of the hallway where it jutted off to the right. But before her, there was a set of stairs leading upward. She bounded up these feeling a little more confident.

A man was coming down around the corner to the left. She dodged sideways with ample time to avoid running into him. He nodded to her and kept about his business. She now found herself on a wide landing.

She turned to her left and started up the second set of stairs. At the top, there were two pathways. Left or right. She guessed her mommy would be down the left one. She was about to head that way when a sudden inclination pulled her attention to the right.

There was nobody down that way putting boxes into the old classrooms. There was nothing down that way. Not even stacks of their belongings. It looked strangely deserted compared to the rest of what she'd experienced so far.

She took a tentative step in that direction. Nothing strange or bad happened, so she took another. Soon she was slowly walking down the deserted hallway. There were two sets of rooms to her left and her right. She guessed there would also be two sets down the left passageway had she gone that way. She knew her mom would be in one of those classrooms already setting up her studio. Ava was sure of it.

She stopped at the first room, immediately to her right. She walked up to the doorway and stared inside. It was empty. She poked her head in and looked to the left.

Once, she imagined, the space would have been filled with desks for children to sit at while the teacher stood up front and lectured about math or history. But now there was nothing.

A cold sensation ran across her shoulders. She lifted a hand and rubbed her right arm. She was surprised that she felt cold. It was July. She pulled away from the classroom, went to the opposite side of the hallway, and looked into that room. It was likewise empty. There was nothing to interest her.

She stared at it for a few seconds, shrugged, then moved to the next classroom on the left side of the hallway. It was just as empty and boring as the first two. She guessed the final classroom would be the same.

When she came to the doorway, she froze. There, sitting in the middle of the classroom, was an old stuffed rabbit doll. It looked dirty and ragged. It had both eyes, but they were dull black glass. Ava tilted her head as she beheld this unexpected phenomenon. She wondered if Mommy or Daddy had placed it there for her to find as a surprise. But by the state of it, she doubted this.

She took a careful step into the classroom and stopped just inside the door. She looked around. There was, of course, no one there to have left the rabbit. But that cold sensation came over her once again, much stronger this time

Her attention went back to the rabbit and stayed there. She carefully strode up to it and crouched before it.

"Hello," she said. "What's your name?"

A broad smile stretched her face, and she giggled. Her eyes traced the long drooping ears.

"I think I will call you Floppy, okay?"

The stuffed rabbit made no response.

She reached a hand forward, took hold of the rabbit, and stood, pressing it to herself, hugging it tightly. "You and I are going to be best friends," Ava said to Floppy.

The promise of a new dolly was forgotten.

3

Mommy

Ava rushed into her mother's studio, clutching her newfound treasure tightly. The little girl located the woman – whose back was to the door – and raced over to her. She beamed with pride, even though the ragged stuffed rabbit smelled a little funny.

"Mommy, Mommy, Mommy!" the girl squealed.

"Just a second, sweety," her mother said. "Mommy's busy right now." She was looking at a piece of paper resting on a clipboard. Ava couldn't understand how Mommy could be even the slightest bit interested in boring old lists when her daughter tried to show her the unbelievable new prize she'd found.

"But Mommy, you have to meet my new *friend!*" Ava whined, punctuating the final word as though it was the most important thing in the world.

"Hold on, Ava!" Mommy replied sharply. "I told you..." Then Mommy stopped talking as she comprehended one part of what her daughter had just said to her. She started to turn as she said, "Friend?"

When she came about Ava thrust the stuffy at her face. Mommy jerked away and raised an arm defensively.

She hissed a curse – one that she had been trying to cut out of her life so that her daughter didn't pick it up – and then said, "Ava! What in the world?"

"This is Floppy!" Ava said.

"Where did you get that filthy thing?" Mommy said, wrinkling her nose. Her back was now pressed against a stack of boxes, preventing her from retreating further.

"In one of the rooms," Ava said, starting to come off the high of finding the rabbit. She was beginning to suspect her mother did not share her delight.

"Why are you... *touching* it?" Mommy said, retreating a step.

Ava tilted her head and wrinkled her nose. Neither of them realized at that moment just how much she resembled her mother. She couldn't understand why Mommy was acting like this about Floppy. This was no way to treat a new friend.

Ava dredged up a memory of something Daddy had said to Mommy on more than one occasion during this move. Mommy had become overwhelmed by the process of packing up all their belongings in preparation to start life in their new home. This resulted in several emotional eruptions. Ava didn't consider that it never seemed to help calm Mommy down, but the girl was at a loss, otherwise.

"Candace, get a hold of yourself!" Ava said, imitating her father's stern tone.

The instant that the change came over her mother's expression, Ava understood she had miscalculated.

"Excuse me, little miss? What did you say to me?"

Ava stood frozen, blinking her large, terrified eyes. She stammered but no words came forth.

Her mother came away from the stack of boxes, her face a darkening thundercloud. She lifted a hand, reaching for Floppy.

"Give me that thing," Mommy said.

That was enough to break the spell of paralysis. Ava's little feet pounded on the wood floor as she attempted an escape. She shook her head violently.

"No!" she howled. "You can't! I just got her. Daddy promised!"

Mommy ceased advancing as an exasperated expression overtook her features. Her lips became a tight, bloodless line. Her eyes blazed with fury, yet something else registered there as well. Ava was too young to understand, but the woman was weighing the potential of compromise. She was also considering having a word with her husband about just what he had promised their daughter.

She had vague recollections of conversations about a new dolly or stuffy. However, she had been too caught up in the details of the move to pay much attention to something that was not truly on her radar of importance. The woman realized she was hunched forward like some cartoon villain and straightened her back. She planted her fists on her hips and mustered as much of a motherly admonishing look as she could manage.

In a calmer voice, she said, "Ava, that thing is so ratty and nasty. I can't let you keep it like that."

Tears brimmed in the little girl's eyes, and she could feel the meltdown working its way up her body. It would reach her face in no time and explode out of her mouth. When that happened there would be no choice but for everyone to ride out the storm.

But her Mommy was wise. She knew just how to deal with the girl before the outburst arrived on the scene.

The woman jutted a finger into the air and an expression communicating full control of the situation appeared on her face.

"But!" she said pointedly. Her eyebrows shot upward, and she paused, allowing the moment to work its full effect on her daughter.

Ava froze, the meltdown halting its progress as a spark of hope blossomed within the little girl. She was frozen like a small animal worried its movement would draw the attention of the nearby predator it sensed.

"We can try to put this... *thing*..."

"Floppy," Ava interrupted, correcting her mother.

Mommy released an exasperated sigh. "...yes, Floppy. We can try to put Floppy through the wash and see if that improves the situation. It will probably have to go through twice, it's so nasty."

Ava's shoulders relaxed as relief washed through her. "Okay!" she said, exhaling the word.

"Mind you," Mommy said, "that thing is so old and ratty looking that it may not survive a couple of trips through the washing machine.

The tide of relief Ava experienced receded a bit. She held Floppy out in front of her and gave the rabbit a worried look. Her eyes flicked back to Mommy as she reconsidered the deal. But she understood it was too late. There would be no backtracking on the solution. It was her only chance at keeping her new stuffy friend.

"Okay," she said again, though with much less enthusiasm. Her attention returned to Mommy, and she gave the woman her best pleading look. "If his arm or ears come off in the wash, we can sew them on again, right?"

"Assuming that's the worst that happens, I suppose," Mommy said. Secretly, Ava's mother harbored the hope that the rabbit would merely disintegrate in the wash. She made a mental note to put the washing machine on its longest and roughest cycle. With any luck, the nasty toy wouldn't be with them for long. She could then swoop in with her husband's promise of another toy and the world would be put right again.

"Can we do it now?" Ava asked. "I want to have Floppy ready for bedtime."

Mommy sighed and cast a glance at all the work of unpacking that lay ahead.

Fortunately, she had the movers put the washer and dryer in place and had her husband slip one of them an extra fifty to get the things properly installed. She knew it would be one of the first things she'd need ready to go. She couldn't stand having days' worth of dirty laundry piling up while they scrambled to figure out the rest of their belongings. Plus, she had a special dinner party coming up and she mustn't be caught unprepared for it.

"Sure," Mommy said. "Let's go get your friend taken care of."

The woman reached out a hand and her daughter smiled widely as she flashed one of her own at her Mommy. Hand in hand, the two of them left the room.

As they set foot into the hallway, Ava's mother was thinking about how lucky she was that she had insisted on the installation of those appliances. Yes, this was looking to be a happy start in their new home.

4

Visitor

Ava practically bounced as they came down the stairs. Her face was stretched in a wide smile that crinkled the flesh at the outer edges of her eyes. Mommy was not quite as happy but was at least pleased to have won something of a minor victory. Or so she thought.

They were now in the lower hallway headed toward the main entrance. Beyond it were what had been the administrative offices and a supply closet once upon a time. In preparation for the family's arrival, the supply closet had been converted into a laundry room and storage place for cleaning supplies and tools.

Before they moved beyond the main entrance an unfamiliar woman's voice called out, "Excuse me?" Mommy slowed to look. Standing several paces yet outside was a face she did not recognize.

The woman was perhaps in her late forties and willowy. Wispy hair with the first hints of gray was pulled back in a bun and carelines stretched the flesh of her face. Inexpertly applied makeup and old clothes probably acquired at a thrift store told the story of a hurried working-class woman on a barely sufficient income. Something danced in her eyes that gave Candace pause.

Ava's mother diverted their course toward her but brought them to a stop just inside the door.

"Hello. Can I help you?"

Ava looked up at her Mommy. She saw an all-too-familiar look on her face. It was the look she gave to people who came to Mommy to hire her for a musical performance, but whom Mommy was likely to decline. It was a shell of politeness but beyond was cold indifference. Ava would never have been able to define this, of course, but she sensed some of it on a rudimentary instinctual level.

"Yes," the woman said taking a few steps closer. She still stopped short of the door, however. Her eyes flicked upward as if looking at something grand and towering. Perhaps the school was this for her, but Candace somehow doubted this. "Are you the person who bought the old school?"

"We are the family who bought it, yes," Ava's Mommy replied.

The woman nodded solemnly, never breaking eye contact. "I see," she said. "May I ask you something?"

"Shoot," Candace replied, blowing a stray lock of hair that had escaped her hair tie out of her face.

The older woman paused, searching for a way to voice what was on her mind. At last, she said, "You seem to be moving a lot of household goods into the school. Why is that?"

Candace shared a marginally confounded look with the woman. She thought, *What kind of question is that? Isn't it obvious?*

She said, "We're moving in. You know... to *live* here?"

The other woman took an involuntary half-step backward and her jaw dropped open as she gaped back at her.

Ava was startled when the woman's gaze shot at her. There was something in the woman's look that unsettled her. Ava crowded her mother's legs, burying her face but then she turned one eye to stare back at the woman.

"You're not serious?" the woman said, looking back at Mommy and giving Ava a minor sense of relief. But until this woman was gone, Ava wouldn't be able to relax. Something about her was scary. Intense.

"I am," Candace said, unperturbed. "It's okay. We've gotten occupancy permits and everything."

"No," the woman said. "That's not it. it's just that…" she trailed off as her gaze flicked beyond them to stare into the old school. She shook her head. "It's just that this used to be my school until they closed it down."

"Oh? Were you a teacher or administrator here?" Ava's mother asked.

"No," the woman said in a distracted voice just above a whisper as she continued to scour the place with her eyes. "Student. It's been closed for a long time."

"Wow," Mommy said, not sounding the least bit enthused. "That must have been a *very* long time ago."

The woman came back to herself. She adopted an affronted expression and said, "It was."

"Look, I get it," Mommy said. "You have a hard time imagining this place could be anything but a school. But it hasn't been one for a long time, as you said. And it won't ever be again. This is my family's home, now, as well as my work studio. Now, if you don't mind..."

The older woman cut her off.

"This is a mistake," she uttered sharply. "No one should live here."

"I understand this may be very emotional for you," Mommy said, "but if you'll just give us a chance..."

"That's not it at all," the woman interrupted again. "I have no fond attachment to this place. Quite the opposite."

"Oh, really?" Candace said. "Could have fooled me. But hey, I get it. If you'd like, maybe after we're settled for a few weeks, you can come back and see what we've done with the place. Put your mind at ease." Candace had no intention of allowing the woman beyond the front door. And she doubted very much the woman would be interested even if the offer were genuine.

"Please listen," the woman said, casting periodic nervous glances at the school, "This place... it isn't safe."

"Of course it is," Candace countered. "We've had it inspected top to bottom. The plumbing is fine, the structure is sound, the electrical could use a little updating but nothing drastic..."

"That's not what I mean," the woman snapped loudly, cutting her off. "I doubt very much you will last four weeks here."

"Honey?" came Ava's Daddy's voice as he strolled up from behind. "Everything okay?" Concern etched his features as a pair of movers stepped around him, carrying a long rug.

"Take that upstairs to the studio," Candace said as they passed her. They grunted in the affirmative and kept moving.

Daddy stood on the opposite side of the walkway leading to the main entrance, eyeing the new woman suspiciously. He shot a questioning look at his wife.

Candace motioned to the woman and said, "Honey, this is apparently one of our new neighbors." She opened her mouth to continue but then realized she was missing a key piece of information. To the woman, she said, "Sorry, I never caught your name."

"Maggie," the woman replied unhappily.

"Yes, Maggie. It turns out Maggie used to attend school here once upon a distant time."

"I'm serious," the older woman said. "This is a dangerous place. You should leave."

Candance affected a bemused disposition and said, "Why, we haven't hardly just got here. I think we'll be fine with staying, thank you."

"If for no other reason than your little girl..." Maggie said, jabbing a crooked finger in Ava's direction. Ava cowered more tightly to her mother's side.

"Mommy?" she said in a quaking voice.

The kind affection now vanished from Candace. "And now we're done. Time for you to leave, *Maggie*."

"This is no game," Maggie pleaded.

"Good thing I'm not in a playful mood," Candace said. "Now get off this property before I have my husband take you by the arm and escort you off. Do you understand?"

Maggie looked helplessly at Candance for a heartbeat or two then turned to look at Candance's husband. She found no haven there. Her countenance grew stony as she turned back to Candance.

"Very well," Maggie said. "But you have been warned." She spared one final cold glance at Candace, then spun around and walked away. One of the movers carrying a large unwieldy box saw her coming just in time and hurriedly sidestepped the woman. He almost lost his balance and his load in the process but righted himself in the end.

"What was *that* about?" Daddy asked.

"Who knows?" his wife replied dismissively. "Local yokel who can't deal with something changing." She lightly pounded her fist on the doorframe and added, "Even if this place hasn't been used in decades."

"Funny how some people get all up in arms about something that isn't theirs," her husband observed.

"Tell me about it," she rolled her eyes. That's when she noticed the pressure on her leg. She looked down and saw that Ava was still clinging ever so tightly to her.

"You okay, kiddo?" she asked.

"She scared me," Ava said.

"I know she did," Mommy replied. "But don't worry. I doubt she'll come back. And even if she does, Daddy will run her off. Right Daddy?" She looked up at her man.

"You bet," he answered with grand confidence. "Nobody scares my little girl without answering to me."

"Really?" Ava said.

"Really, babe," Daddy replied.

"Now how about we go see about getting your friend washed up?" Mommy said.

The girl instantly transformed from a terrified wilting flower to an exuberant freight train of delight. Ava squealed and stepped away from her mother's leg, displaying Floppy to her father for the first time.

"Hey, who's this? I don't recognize this one, do I?"

"Long story," Mommy said. "I'll tell you later."

"Okay, well, I suppose I should oversee the last loads being brought in. The piano will come last. And let me tell you – am I ever glad we've got all these movers to deal with that thing! Getting it upstairs with just the two of us would be a beast. Probably impossible."

"Alright, my love," Mommy said, giving Daddy one of their intimate looks. "Catch up with you later."

"Better believe it," Daddy said, giving her a wink and leaning in for a quick kiss.

"Yuck!" Ava said.

"Hey, keep that up and we won't be able to get you that little brother you keep begging us for!" Daddy said with another wink at Mommy.

"What does gross kissing have to do with getting me a baby brother?" Ava asked, sounding disgusted.

"Nothing at all, my sweet," Daddy said with a throaty laugh. "Nothing at all."

Ava gave her Daddy a confused look, then turned to her mother for help. Mommy just shrugged, but Ava thought the woman suppressed a laugh.

Grownups are weird, she thought as Mommy led her to the washing machine.

5

CRASH

Floppy was still warm from his journey through the laundry machine and dryer when Ava and Mommy sat down to dinner. The little stuffed rabbit only looked a little better in Mommy's opinion, but at least its smell was much improved. Ava didn't really care one way or the other. She was just happy to have her new friend so close after waiting an eternity for it to be cleaned.

There were still countless boxes everywhere they looked, some open and only half emptied of their contents. But they had made time to set up the table. Three wooden chairs surrounded the circular table, only two of which were currently occupied.

"Is Daddy gonna be home soon?" Ava asked.

"Any minute," Mommy replied in a half-interested tone as she stared at her phone. "Just hold your horses, little miss."

Ava heaved an exasperated sigh. She was not very patient. But then what six-year-old is? This was their first night in a new place and she was anxious. So, Mommy and Daddy had made a few rock-solid promises (or so they called them) to help ease some of the girl's difficulty. The first of which was that their initial family meal in their new home would be pizza from a local place. None of the chain restaurants with which they were familiar were close enough. One pizza was half everything for Mommy and the other half only meat for Daddy. The other pizza was to be plain cheese per Ava's desires.

Ava tossed an exasperated expression toward the front door. Large windows with wood latticework showed an empty walkway. She had hoped to see her father striding up with their dinner. None of the local places delivered so he had to run into town to get it himself.

"Just chill," Mommy said. "He'll be here soon."

Ava looked at Mommy. "And then?"

"Yes," Mommy said in an exhausted tone, still not looking at her daughter. "We'll have our pizza and watch *The Princess Bride*."

That was the other conciliation Mommy and Daddy had made. It was Ava's favorite movie. Although, she didn't like the part with the giant rats. They had to fast-forward through that part for her. Still, her favorite movie and her favorite dinner had already gone a long way to alleviate the child's concerns. But not all of them.

Ava's mind turned toward the spacious upstairs and the two darkened hallways they had left behind half an hour ago. Mommy's studio was to be up there, but they would all sleep on the ground floor. They had already chosen a room for Mommy and Daddy and one for Ava. For now, the rest of the upstairs would be empty. But Daddy envisioned a business office in one of the other rooms for himself and perhaps they would rent out some of the other spaces. The multiple rooms were one of the main facets that had attracted them to purchase the old school.

Ava turned around to look out the big windows facing the walkway. Just then something odd caught her attention. She saw three heads reflected in the glass. Hers, Mommy's, and what she had at first assumed was Daddy approaching from the outside. But then her eyes adjusted and told her the walkway was still empty. She tilted her head and scrunched up her face as she stared. Then it dawned on her that there should not be a third person in the cafeteria with them.

She gasped and spun around, searching the room. Mommy had been looking at her phone, *doom scrolling* as Daddy called it. The sudden noise of surprise from her daughter startled her and she dropped the device. It clattered on the table, then teetered, almost falling to the floor. Mommy drew a sharp surprised breath, placing a hand on her chest. Mommy turned her face to Ava. Wide eyes stared at the little girl.

"What?" she barked.

Ava ignored Mommy for a moment. Her little head darted back and forth, her eyes scouring the scene. But there was no one else. She turned a confused expression on her mother.

"*What?*" Mommy repeated, more insistent.

"I thought I saw…" Ava started but trailed off.

Mommy lifted her eyes to the doorway, assuming the girl meant her father. When she found the doorway vacant her shoulders relaxed, and she turned accusing eyes on her little girl.

"Don't do that!" she said. "You nearly gave me a coronary."

Ava tilted her head and said, "A what?"

Mommy waved her hands. "Never mind," she said reaching for her phone. She picked up the device, thumbed it back to life, and continued her distracting activity.

Ava slowly turned her attention back to the doorway and stared at the reflection in the glass. This time she counted only two heads. She was certain she had seen three before. But then again, Mommy and Daddy frequently said she had a strong imagination. Maybe she had made it up.

Nevertheless, she hugged Floppy tightly as she turned away from the doorway.

She fell silent.

A few minutes later, Daddy burst through the front doors bearing two steaming boxes.

"TA-DA!" he announced with a flourish.

"Oh, thank goodness," Mommy said. "I'm starving."

A broad smile stretched Ava's face, and she began to wriggle and bounce in her seat. The scent of the pizza reached her and banished any recollection of seeing another person in the room.

"Yay!" she shouted. Daddy swaggered over to the table, depositing the stacked pizza boxes in the center like a waiter at a fancy restaurant. He was careful to avoid the plates and cups. The cups were filled with water and mostly melted ice cubes. Beads of condensation had formed on the outside of the cups. Ava had complained, asking why they couldn't have pop instead.

The standard answer came. It was much too late for her to be drinking anything like that.

They had a long day, true. It was already after eight o'clock, normally well after Ava's bedtime. But tonight was special. She got to stay up, have her pizza, and watch her favorite movie.

Both Mommy and Daddy were certain the girl would be asleep within ten minutes once the movie started. Yet they didn't say anything. Then the girl would be whisked off to bed where she would awaken the next morning. That was the plan, anyway.

The pizza was parceled out and the family dug in.

They weren't more than a couple of bites into their dinner when a loud crash resounded from overhead. The family all froze and darted their eyes between one another. Then, as if they were a single organism, their eyes drifted toward the ceiling.

Daddy swallowed and said, "What was that?"

Mommy's back straightened as she pushed away from the table, then stood. She sent a dark look beyond the confines of the old cafeteria, at the stairs leading to the next level.

"I'll tell you what it is," she said. "Those idiot movers we paid too much for stacked boxes like I specifically told them not to. I'm sure something important is broken."

"We better go have a look," Daddy said with resignation. He spared his partially eaten slice of pizza a longing look then pushed away from the table.

"Better come with us kiddo," Daddy said, extending a hand to Ava.

Ava shoved a big bite of pizza in her face, tore it off, and started chewing as she also pushed away from the table. She reached up and took her father's hand.

Daddy grinned as he took Ava's hand, and they set off after Mommy. The woman moved ahead of them like a shark gliding through nighttime waters. She marched up the stairs with pounding footfalls. Daddy and Ava struggled to keep up with her.

They followed her as she turned the corner and went up the second set of stairs. She raced down the hallway toward her studio. She didn't bother to turn on the upstairs lights. Daddy stopped at the top and turned on the bank of switches to illuminate the hallway housing her new studio. Then they followed after Mommy.

She was already at the doorway leading into her studio which was still far from set up. She reached into the room and flicked on the light switch. She planted her fists on her hips as her gaze swept the room. Even from the side and behind her a little, they could see the dark look she sported. When they came up right behind her, Daddy leaned in.

"Doesn't look like there's anything wrong here," he said. "Maybe it was one of the other rooms?"

Mommy didn't respond but stepped into the space to get a better look. Daddy followed her. And, by virtue of him still holding onto Ava's hand, so did she. Mommy's face darted around the room until it landed in a corner.

"There," she growled, jabbing a finger. Three quick steps later she stood over a stack of boxes. Daddy and Ava followed her until they saw the tipped-over box with its contents spilled onto the floor.

Mommy growled as she crouched by the mess.

"This mixer had better not be broken, or I swear I'll have someone's head." Sitting on the floor cattywampus was a small sound mixer.

"It'll take a while to get everything set up before we can find out," Daddy said scratching his head with his free hand.

Mommy muttered several angry things under her breath, none of which Ava caught. Which was probably for the best. When Mommy got like this, she tended to use naughty words that she didn't want Ava repeating.

Ava stared at Mommy with tense shoulders, uncertain if an explosion was to follow. Sometimes when Mommy got upset, that anger ended up being directed at her. Even if she had nothing to do with it. Or sometimes even Daddy bore the brunt of it. She felt the man's grip on her hand tense ever so slightly. He knew it too.

Ava looked away from Mommy to the windows outside. Soon there would be sound-proof panels on wood boards to cover the windows. They were stacked in a corner, waiting for someone to install them.

She couldn't see outside very well since the lights were turned on and it was dark out there. All she saw was a reflection of the contents and occupants of the room. There was herself and her Daddy standing there... and then something else drew her eye. There was another figure standing in the doorway behind them. She gasped and spun. When she came about the doorway was empty.

"What?" Mommy snapped.

"Take it easy," Daddy said to Mommy.

"She was like this earlier," Mommy said, motioning to Ava with her chin, unable to hide her frustration. "So jumpy."

"I don't think she's the jumpy one," Daddy observed with a hint of accusation. Mommy glowered at Daddy, but Daddy stood his ground. Ava didn't catch any of that. She was too busy staring at the doorway where she was certain someone stood moments ago. She kept expecting whoever it was to appear. But there shouldn't be anyone else in their new home. She knew that, too. Maybe that was why such a sense of dread constricted her little heart.

"Well, there's nothing we can do about this now," Daddy said. "What's done is done. If there's anything broken, I'm sure I can wrangle the moving company into paying the damages. It definitely is their fault."

This seemed to at least blunt the edge of Mommy's anger. She grunted and stood.

"All right," she replied, not sounding all right. "I suppose you're right." She huffed an exasperated sigh, shook her head, then said, "Well dinner's getting cold. We better get back to it."

"I couldn't agree more," Daddy said. He turned to Ava and said, "Ready, babe?"

Ava turned a confused look at Daddy. She hadn't been paying attention to anything they said. She had been too consumed with what she thought she saw.

"What, Daddy?"

"Let's go downstairs and get some grub," he said. "Then we can start your movie."

"Right," Ava said absently as she turned to stare at the vacant doorway once more. "Okay, let's go."

6

BED

To her parents' surprise, Ava made it almost to the very end of the movie. It was far enough that they let her slumber, cuddled up to Daddy's side while they let the rest of the adventure play out. With the princess rescued and the little girl dozing softly, Daddy gently scooped the girl up and made his way toward her room.

Her little arms clung tightly to Floppy which caused Mommy to frown. She was already conspiring how she might extricate the mangy thing from her daughter. She didn't care how many wash cycles the thing endured: the rabbit was *persona non grata* as far as Mommy was concerned.

But she also already feared that any attempt to divest them of the ragged stuffy would be too little, too late. The girl loved the thing. *L-O-V-E-D* it.

Mommy's arms folded across her chest as she watched her husband carry the girl and her fuzzy companion away.

In a rare moment of self-reflection, she stopped to ask herself why she was so set against her daughter keeping the stuffed animal. After all, what harm could it really cause? She had doused the thing with disinfectant, and it sat soaking in the stuff before it had gone into the washing machine for the first, then a second time. It would be ridiculous to consider that the girl might catch something unsavory from the abandoned toy. And any parasite or insect that had dwelt behind its vacant glassy eyes and within its ancient stuffing was surely dead now.

Still, she didn't like the thing.

A chill ran over her shoulders and a shudder coursed through her as she witnessed her husband disappear around the corner leading into Ava's room. She rubbed her bare arms to dispel the cold sensation.

A goose walked over your grave, she heard her mother's voice in her head. That unwelcome intrusion was worse than the advent of their surprise stuffed housemate. It had been a while since she thought of her mother and the woman's cavalcade of unsupportive admonishments regarding her choice of career, husband, and just about anything else she could think of.

They hadn't talked in... God, how long? Three years. Yes, that's it. Since Ava turned three. That was right around the time that Candance's music had begun to gain traction. Sure, it was still just a gig at a local dive here, a sale of a few albums there. But it was the start of something good. She could feel it.

But not as far as her mother was concerned.

She esteemed Candace's musical aspirations to be worth not much at all.

Then why did you shove me into all those classes and recitals? she recalled shouting at her mother in accusation.

Not so you could waste your life chasing a silly dream, her mother shouted back.

That delightful shouting match had been at Ava's third birthday party, right before the cake with three tiny candles was to be brought out. It had made things with their friends... awkward.

I don't want to argue about this now, Candace had said, picking up the cake and turning away.

Running away as always, I see, her mother had replied. Then in a pleasant little jab, she added, *Just like your useless father*.

She had felt her back go rigid and icy as she halted her retreat. She slowly spun to look at the victorious glint in her mother's eyes. The ice turned to ire as she felt fire rising from her gut. A volcanic eruption was seconds away. But she stopped herself. She vowed not to ruin her daughter's birthday further.

In a calm and cool tone, she replied, *No, mother. I don't run from you. And neither did Daddy. You drove him away*. She took a measured step in her mother's direction and in a confidential manner stated, *Just like you are driving me away. And if you don't want me close to you, then I will oblige. The door's over there.* She nodded with her chin toward the front of the house.

A small but stunned audience waited in the dining room around the table by then. Among them was her husband who had battled within himself whether to step to his wife's side in her defense. In the end, he elected to hold back. He had known this was a long time coming and suspected she needed to handle this on her own.

She watched her mother spin in a huff and storm toward the front door. She stood frozen like that for a long while after the woman had disappeared through the door. The candles had melted halfway to the frosting when her husband came to stand by her side. He put a hand on her shoulder and gently squeezed.

She snapped out of it and jerked her face toward him, having not realized he was there until that moment. A relieved breath rolled out of her when she saw him giving her a weak, conciliatory smile. A tear rolled down her cheek in reply and he reached up to wipe it away. Together, they turned and headed to the dining room to rejoin the party.

Three years later, Candace found herself reliving the unpleasant memory and a fresh tear coursed its way down her cheek.

When Mike returned from depositing Ava and Floppy in her bed, he wore a self-satisfied smile. The expression vanished like a puff of candle smoke in a gale when he beheld the haunted expression on his wife's face.

"Hey, everything okay?" he asked, striding up to her quickly.

She dropped her face and rubbed the tear away from her cheek.

"Fine," she lied.

"You sure?" he asked with a healthy dose of caution. "You don't seem fine."

She lifted her face again, bearing a forced look of pleasantry. "Sure," she said. "Everything's just hunky-dory." She turned to stare off at some undetermined point in space and muttered, "It's just...." She trailed off and he waited, not wanting to prompt her if she wasn't ready to deal with whatever this was. At last, she added, "I was just thinking of my mother."

"Ah," Mike said. "It's been a while, hasn't it? What brought her up this time?"

She shook her head. "It's the weirdest thing. I was just watching you carry Ava to bed, and I was thinking about how to get rid of her new ratty treasure..."

"The rabbit?" he interjected in disbelief. "What's wrong with the rabbit?"

She hemmed and hawed. She said, "Nothing, I guess. It just doesn't feel... I just don't like it."

Mike cocked his head to one side and said, "But how did you get from the rabbit to your mom?"

She tossed her shoulders up in a defeated shrug. "Couldn't say. At one second, I was thinking of the rabbit, and the next thing I knew..."

This time he did finish the thought for her. "The old battle-ax sprang to mind."

"I guess so."

"That must be some kind of record for a leap in logic. What do you think about trying out for the Olympics in the Long Jump?" He dropped her a wink and a smirk, but she wasn't having it.

"I think I'll pass," she replied dryly.

The two of them fell silent as the moment dragged on. Mike was the one to break it.

"What do you say we turn in, ourselves? It's been a long day, and we've got loads to do tomorrow."

"Works for me," Candance said.

***

The blackest darkness she'd ever experienced enveloped her as she came awake. Ava had no way of knowing it was three o'clock in the morning as there was no bedside alarm clock in her room. She hadn't awakened at that hour since she was a baby in need of feeding. And she couldn't say what exactly had yanked her back to consciousness this time.

She just knew something was wrong.

Her little eyes fluttered open and were met by approximately the same amount of darkness as when her eyes had remained closed. She sat up slowly and turned her head carefully to take in the benighted room.

Soon her eyes adjusted, and moonlight filtered into her space from behind the large custom blinds Mommy and Daddy had installed before they moved in. The dim light wasn't much help with defining her environment, but it was better than the utter nothingness that greeted her upon waking.

The room was flooded with shadows and dark shapes. If it had been daylight, she would have discerned these as piles of boxes and her bedroom furniture. But in the dark, they appeared as mute, threatening shapes that might reach out at any moment to grab and eat her.

She felt cold… very cold. A shiver ran through her and she groped around the bed, feeling for Floppy. But Floppy wasn't there. With each pat of her hand on the rumpled surface of the covers she grew more desperate.

Her breaths came quicker. She leaned forward and reached toward the extremities of her legs. Still, there was no sign of her new best friend.

She got up to her knees and pushed the covers aside. She put her hands on the edge of her bed and looked beyond it. She just hoped she wouldn't be greeted with the bright yellow glowing eyes of some monster that made its home under her bed. There were no eyes, no monster... and no Floppy.

She realized she couldn't remember going to bed. She must have fallen asleep and been carried in here. But Mommy and Daddy wouldn't have forgotten her new friend, would they? Well, she thought Mommy might. She didn't seem to like Floppy very much, though Ava couldn't fathom why.

She searched the room, perched atop her bed like an eagle rooted at the highest peak of a tree, looking for a tasty animal to snatch. But it was so dark that...

That's when she thought she saw the momentary reflection of two eyes, standing in the corner of her room. They were attached to a vague shape that was only slightly darker than the shadows surrounding it.

Ava's heart seemed to stop, and her face went warm and tingly. The skin of her cheeks felt heavy, sort of droopy, even. Her breath caught in her little lungs.

The eyes flashed again, this time a little longer as the head of the person to whom those eyes belonged tilted his head.

That's when Ava screamed bloody murder.

7

Intruder

Nothing wakes up a father like the unmitigated terrified shrieks of his little girl. Mike threw aside the covers and was out of bed in three seconds flat. His head was still clearing of sleep by the time he had taken his first step, flowing into action by instinct alone. By the time he was two steps away, he had taken in the almost pitch-dark nature of his environment and reason started to take over. But only a little.

The third step was more cautious, but the continued noise of Ava's shrieks cascaded through his veins with rocket fuel. He shuffled toward what he judged to be the doorway.

"Wha...?" Candace moaned from the bed, just pushing herself up on her elbow. "What's going on?"

Ava shrieked again and the woman's motherly nature brought her fully awake with a snap. "Ava?" she said.

Mike didn't bother responding. He found the door and pulled it open. There was far more moonlight in the hallway. Pale blue illumination showed him the way.

His bare feet slapped on the cold tile floor as he dashed toward his daughter's room.

"Ava?" he yelled. "Daddy's coming!"

He arrived at the door to her room and pushed it open. He fumbled along the wall just inside until he found the light switches. Piercing brilliance caused him to wince and draw back momentarily.

"Daddy!" Ava cried. "Daddy, he's going to get me!"

Mike barged into the room, his attention darting everywhere for the threat. He found none.

His attention landed on Ava who sat up in her bed, her back pressed against the headboard and wall. Her gaze was fixed on a point in the room. He whipped around to see what she might be staring at. He discerned nothing that should have caused such a reaction in his little girl.

He shuffled over to her bed and sat.

"Baby, what's wrong?" he said, reaching for her. She didn't wait for his hand to arrive. She dived for him and wrapped her arms around his neck.

"Daddy, the man was going to get me!"

"Man?" came Candance's voice from the doorway. Mike swiveled his head to take in the exhausted form of his wife leaning on the doorframe. "What man?"

"The man in the corner, the man in the dark," Ava blurted but the words were muffled as her face was buried in her father's shoulder.

"There's no one here," Mike said. "Just look, Baby."

He turned, bearing her whole form around so he no longer obstructed her view. She lifted her head and stared at the corner where she had seen… something? Someone? She was sure there had been two piercing eyes floating in the dark. But now there was no sign of anything.

"Where did he go?" Ava asked through a hitching voice.

Mike answered, "Baby, I don't think anyone was in here with you. I think you just had a bad dream."

"Are you sure about that?" Candace asked from the door.

Mike shot her an *are-you-kidding-me-right-now?* look. But Candace was staring at the same corner with which Ava seemed so preoccupied. He followed her gaze and noticed something peculiar for the first time.

Resting atop a stack of boxes was Ava's new stuffed rabbit friend, Floppy. Mike distinctly recalled the girl holding it to herself as he carried her and laid her in bed hours ago. How had the thing gotten across the room? That didn't matter to him, though, as he thought understood part of his daughter's night terror.

"Baby, look. It's just your friend."

Mike felt a jolt of surprise rush through Ava.

"Floppy?" she asked. "How did you get over there?" She let go of Mike's neck and hopped down from the bed. She rushed over to the stack of boxes and stared at the stuffy perched atop them. She reached a hand toward her new friend but then hesitated.

"That's what you saw in the dark, kiddo. It wasn't someone in your room. It was just your rabbit."

Candace shot Mike a look.

"Why did you leave the rabbit over there?" she asked.

"I didn't," he answered. "She had a death grip on the thing when I laid her down. It was with her when I left the room."

Candance narrowed her eyes at him, stared at him for a few seconds longer, and then shifted her focus back to her daughter. "Weird," was all she said.

Mike surmised Ava must have gotten up in the middle of the night to go to the bathroom and put the stuffy on the boxes for safekeeping. Maybe she even sleepwalked doing it. That was something she'd done a few times when she was younger. But it had been a while. He'd hash it out with Candace in the morning.

"Okay, little miss," Candace said. "Get your friend and let's get you back into bed."

Ava whipped around and gave her mother a terrified look.

"You're not going to make me sleep in here all by myself, are you?"

"Baby, this is your room," Mike said. "That's what it's for. You had your own room at the old apartment. This isn't any different."

Candance cleared her throat. Mike turned to her and raised his eyebrows.

She said, "Maybe you should have a look around. Just in case."

"In case of what?"

In a whisper not low enough to hide what she was saying from their daughter, Candace said, "What if someone else is in here? What if squatters are hiding in the place?"

Ava whimpered. She snatched Floppy from the top of the box and scurried to her mother's side.

Mike heaved an exasperated sigh. He was about to argue when he discerned the adamant nature of the look his wife was giving him.

"Okay," he relented. "Just let me get dressed."

"And take a baseball bat or something," Candance hissed. "Just in case there really is someone else here."

"Baseball bat?" Mike replied incredulously. "When have you ever known me to own a baseball bat? Or any other sports equipment for that matter?"

"I don't care about other sports crap," she snapped back. "I'm not asking you to play catch with our home invaders. I'm asking you to beat them until they go away."

Mike grunted. "Fine. I'll grab one of your music stands from upstairs."

A truncated noise of protest squeaked out of Candace, and she put a clenched fist to her mouth as she scrunched up her face.

"What is it now?" he asked.

Candace sucked a quick breath through gritted teeth, then said, "Just... not one of the nice, new ones, okay?"

He sighed. "Fine. I'll grab a ratty beat-up one. Happy?"

She seemed to relax a little at that.

He stood from the bed and lumbered toward the door. As he passed Candace and Ava, he muttered, "If I'm not back in ten minutes, I've probably run away and joined the circus. Somewhere I'll be appreciated."

8

Dog

Nine minutes later, Mike returned to his room where he found Candace and Ava snuggled together, but sitting up. He still carried the older music stand he'd promised to take with him for protection.

"Well?" his wife said.

"It's just us," Mike replied. "As I suspected, we can all sleep safe and sound in our *own* beds tonight." His emphasis on the word 'own' was pointed at his wife. She received the message loud and clear but shook her head vehemently.

"I think Ava will do better to stay with us for the night," she said. She arched an eyebrow as if to lay a challenge before her husband. He was too tired to rise to it, however.

He nodded and said, "Sure whatever. But it's late so we need to get right back to sleep. We've got a lot of unpacking to do tomorrow."

Candance and Ava shifted to make room for him. Mike grumbled to himself and set the music stand down inside the room. He turned, closed the door, and flicked off the lights. A moment later he was sliding under the covers and adjusting until he was laid out as he preferred.

"Goodnight Mommy, goodnight Daddy," Ava said.

"Goodnight sweetheart," Candance said in a sweet and clear voice.

"Goodnight, baby," Mike mumbled.

It wasn't long after that Ava found herself wedged between two snoring adults. She couldn't understand how they could fall asleep so fast after what had happened. She was still sure she had seen someone in her room and that it hadn't merely been Floppy.

For one thing, she'd gone to sleep holding onto the rabbit for dear life. She hadn't put him on top of those boxes. Someone had to have taken him from her. But who?

She was certain it was the same person she had seen staring at her in her room. But where had that person gone? And who were they?

Ava was too uneasy to fall asleep right away like her parents did. Thus, she found herself awake in the dark again. At least this time she had Mommy and Daddy right there with her and if she thought someone came into the room, she could wake them and let them know. Maybe then Daddy would be able to catch whoever it was.

She lay between her parents for a long time, listening to the strange creaking noises of their new home. It was different than the apartment they had lived in before. That place had its noises, too, obviously, but the ones here seemed deeper, bigger... hollower. Scarier, in other words.

Ava was no good at judging the time, but it was about an hour later when she began her slow descent into the haze of sleep-land once more. Just before she slipped out of consciousness, Ava was overcome by the sensation of being watched by keenly interested eyes. It was too late for her to raise an alarm for her parents. It was too late for her to do anything for herself. That feeling colored her every sleeping moment and troubled her dreams.

In them, she was being chased through the streets by a dark beast, a big black dog. She kept crying out for her Daddy. She could even hear him calling back to her, asking her where she was. But she didn't know. She couldn't tell him.

Then, up ahead she saw Floppy standing in the middle of the street. He raised an arm and waved at her in greeting. She raced toward him, crying terrified tears. She wished he would bounce to her help. But he just stood there, waving.

"Floppy!" she cried. "Help!"

But he only stood and waved, stood and waved, stood and...

She was forced to the ground, the pavement ripping into her skin. She'd skinned her knees a few times while learning to ride her bike. Oh, how that had hurt. But this was worse. It was all over.

Her dream world was red with agony and the pavement ground at her from one side and the big black dog got her from the other.

She opened her mouth to scream, staring with betrayed eyes at Floppy. She reached out to him. Instead of coming to her aid, the stuffed rabbit turned and sauntered slowly away.

"Floppy, please!" Ava screamed.

"Ava!" her Daddy's voice was closer now. "Ava, time to get up, Baby."

"Daddy, help!" she screamed. The dog kept at her, pinning her to the street and biting into her poor little back. "It's getting me!"

Then the dog was gone from her back, and she flew up toward the starlit sky. She flew like a superhero, though she had no control over it. But it was a relief, nevertheless.

"Come on, Baby, time for…"

Then her dark world went bright.

She was awake and blinded by the light. Big warm arms enveloped her.

"…breakfast," Daddy said.

Ava started thrashing, not understanding what was going on. Her Daddy held her tight, though.

"Hey, hey, it's okay Baby. It's just me."

Ava's eyes came open at last and she beheld the face of her father.

"Daddy?" she said.

"Yep, just me, pumpkin. You ready for some eggs and toast?"

Ava blinked several times, then her arms stretched out and an involuntary yawn escaped her. She blinked a few more times, and said, "Daddy, where am I?"

"You slept in our bed last night, remember?"

"I was outside," she said, confused.

"Must have been dreaming, kiddo," he said.

"It was… scary," she said.

"Sure," he replied. "You had a fright in your bed last night. You thought your rabbit was a person in your room. You screamed and screamed until Daddy came and saved you. Remember?"

Her brow furrowed as she stared at him. She recalled most of what he said. But something about what it wasn't right. Yet she couldn't remember what.

"Hey, I'll even throw in some bacon to sweeten the deal. What do you say?"

"Bacon?" the girl's eyes lit up.

"That's Daddy's girl!" Daddy said with a laugh. "Let's go."

Ava looked down and saw that she still held Floppy. That was a relief. She didn't want to leave him alone if someone else was hiding in their new home who liked to go around and move stuff... or take what wasn't theirs.

As they exited Mommy and Daddy's room, she looked around to make sure no one was lingering in a corner.

A few seconds later as they approached the cafeteria-turned-dining-room, Ava said, "Daddy?"

"Yes, my love?" he said.

She hesitated, then, thinking about her dream, said, "I don't want to get a dog."

He paused and looked at her.

"What do you mean, kiddo?"

"I don't like dogs. I don't want to get a dog."

He eyed her suspiciously, wondering what on earth had brought this on. But in the back of his mind, he found a sense of relief. He thought that strange, since he'd grown up with a dog and loved that old pooch. But considering the dream he'd had last night – one where he'd been chased by a big black dog – he didn't exactly feel pet-friendly at the moment.

"Okay, Baby, whatever you say. No dogs for us. Just eggs and bacon." He smirked at her and wiggled a finger in her side, tickling her.

She giggled.

Two Dead at Old School

The following is a selection of an article from the Cedar Park Herald, a local newspaper. Dated January 15, 1997

Nearly a decade after tragedy struck at the once proud Cedar Park School, history seems to have repeated itself.

On Tuesday, January 14th, police responded to a disturbance reported by a neighbor at the abandoned building of the old school.

The facility is known to have electrical problems with lights periodically flickering off and on in the middle of the night throughout the old building, visible from outside. However, the nature of this particular disturbance was not merely a repeat of these mundane problems. The sounds of shattering glass and screams were heard after 10 p.m. on the night of the 14th.

Responding officers came upon a grisly scene. Two mutilated bodies were recovered in one of the old classrooms.

The pair, and probably a third individual, broke into the old school sometime over the last several days and appear to have intended to squat. That intention ended in violence.

Both recovered victims were adults; one man and one woman. They bore no identification.

A set of bloody footprints leads away from the victims and to a shattered window. No evidence outside the building indicates anyone exited that way. Nor is there any sign of who made the footprints or where they might have gone.

More on this story as it develops.

9

Setup

Mommy sat at the table which looked ridiculously tiny given the size of the cafeteria. None of them had paid much attention the night before because it was dark and everyone was tired. But now that daylight had encroached and the tide of tiredness was ebbing away, Mommy and Daddy at least had gained a bit of perspective.

"This space is really going to need a few things to make it feel like home, you know?" Mommy remarked when Daddy brought Ava into the room. There were numerous boxes scattered about the spacious room as there were in most of the rest of the rooms. But these did little to dispel the sense of vacancy. The grown-ups knew the sense would only increase once everything had found its proper home. They had moved from a three-bedroom apartment as well as carted contents from a rented storage unit and though they had numerous belongings, the stacks of boxes were no match for the great swathes of emptiness presented by the one-time school.

Daddy nodded thoughtfully as he deposited Ava into her seat, then headed over to the stove. He opened the refrigerator and began removing breakfast items.

"Yeah," he said. "But that's second-order-of-business stuff. If you're serious about having people over next week, we have to bust our butts getting what we already have squared away. I know you don't want them waltzing into a pig stye."

Mommy's cheek twitched.

"Hey, don't go sour on me," Daddy said. "That was your call to make two months ago. It's too late to back out now without looking like a bunch of chumps. And I don't need to remind you that that's the last thing we want to look like with these people."

Mommy released a sigh as her shoulders sagged and she propped herself up on the table with her elbows. "I know, I know," she said. "It's just so much closer now, you know?"

"You don't have to tell me," Daddy replied. "I'm the one who keeps track of the calendar. You're the artsy, whimsical type. Right?"

Mommy waved a dismissive hand. "Yeah, yeah," she said. "I just don't know how I'm supposed to get the house in order as well as get my studio up and running by the end of next week. It's impossible."

"Enough of that," Daddy said with a smirk. He turned and winked at Ava. She returned an exaggerated one at him.

"We can do it, Mommy," she said.

Mommy favored the girl with a weak smile. "Thanks, sweetheart," she said. "We'll try our best, won't we?"

"Look, don't sweat it," Daddy said. "They were working to get those soundproofing boards put together and electrical updated weeks ago. It should take us three days tops to get the soundproof boards up over the windows and the studio equipment up and running. Maybe another day to work the kinks out. After that, it's fine-tuning. That leaves plenty of time to work on the rest of the place."

"I know," she said, sinking lower toward the table. It just has to be kind of perfect, you know?"

"You want to make an impression, I get it," Daddy replied. "But hey, don't forget that good impressions are my specialty."

Mommy straightened her back and gave him a patronizing look. "Is that so?" she volleyed at him.

"I won you over, didn't I?" he answered with a smirk.

"Pfft, barely," she answered but Ava noticed her cheeks were pinking up.

A spike of concern arose in the girl, and she said, "Mommy, what's wrong with your face? Do you have a fever?"

Daddy cleared his throat noisily and played on his daughter's concern, his grin widening. "Yeah, Mommy what's wrong with your face?"

Mommy turned her face away and waved them off. "Oh, shut up," she said with a little giggle.

***

Breakfast was behind them and work was ahead.

As Mommy wiped Ava's face, she asked, "Who do you want to help this morning, Babe? Mommy or Daddy?"

"Can't I explore?"

Mommy's eyes briefly shot to Daddy then returned to the girl. "No, that's a bad idea. This is a big place for such a little person, and I don't want you accidentally getting into something you shouldn't."

"But I've got Floppy to watch me," Ava said. However, even as the words came out something stirred in her memory. Something she couldn't quite grasp. Something about a street and her needing help... and Floppy standing there and not helping. But it was elusive.

"Thanks, Floppy," Daddy said, addressing the ragged stuffy, "but I think you and Ava need to hang with one of us. So, how about it, kiddo? Which will it be?"

Ava scratched her chin for a moment then said, "Daddy!"

Mommy expelled a defeated breath and shook her head. With a false frown, she said, "Why is it always Daddy?"

"Because Daddy is big, strong, and handsome," Daddy pronounced. "I thought you would have figured that out by now."

"Fine," Mommy replied with exaggerated deference. "I suppose I'll just slave away in the salt mines alone, singing my old-timey work songs."

"Hey, I bet that would make a great Instagram reel," Daddy said, nudging her with an elbow.

"Ha-ha," she replied dryly. "You're hilarious."

He shrugged. "I do what comes naturally. It works."

"Okie-dokie," she said, turning serious. "I'll head upstairs and get cracking on the studio. You two can start in here, I suppose. it's one of the first things people see when they come in."

Ava had stopped paying attention to them. Something outside caught her notice. There was a flash of movement near the front door, but she couldn't tell if it was on the inside or the outside. So, she stared that way, hoping to catch a glimpse of it again.

She was about to give up when it returned. A boy's face briefly appeared outside the door. He stared in, looking around. he was about Ava's size and dark-haired. She couldn't see much more than that.

"Daddy, look a boy!"

But Daddy was too interested in Mommy. Ava glanced at them and got the feeling the two of them were about to start smooching again. *Bleck, no thank-you,* she thought. She shifted her gaze back to the boy and found him staring directly at her. He peered at her with exceptionally wide eyes. It startled her.

Her mouth dropped open, and she raised a hand and waved tentatively at him. But the boy just kept staring at her. A swelling ball of unease formed in her gut.

"Daddy?" she said, not taking her eyes off the kid staring at her.

"Yeah, Baby?" he replied but he was still trading looks with Mommy.

"There's a strange boy outside who keeps looking at me," she said.

"Sounds like you found a winner," Mommy said. "There's a strange boy in her that keeps staring at me, too, but I'm stuck with him."

Ava turned to her father at last and tugged on his sleeve. "Daddy, will you look, please?"

"Sure thing, kiddo," he said. "Where is this kid?" He turned and tracked where his daughter was pointing. But when Ava returned her focus to the front door the boy was no longer there.

"He's gone," she said.

Daddy shrugged. "Probably just got bored," he said. "We can talk to him if he comes back and knocks, though, okay?"

"Talk to him?" Ava asked, worry edging her tone.

"Yeah, that's generally how people make friends," Daddy said. "And this is a new place for us, so we're going to have to make new friends, right?"

"I miss my old friends," Ava said. Her face screwed up in concentration as she tried to remember the faces of her regular playgroup.

"I know, Baby," Mommy said. "But Daddy's right. We get to meet new people now."

Ava shot a glance at the door leading outside again. It remained vacant but her sense of unease persisted.

"Okay," she said. "I guess." But the more she thought about it, the less certain she was that she wanted to meet the boy. She'd only seen him from a distance and for such a short time. But that little bit of eye contact made her skin feel... cold.

10

Explore

The next day was just as full and non-stop as move-in day had been. Daddy spent a lot of time going through boxes and muttering things to himself. More than once, he asked no one in particular how a certain item had gotten into whatever box he had found it in. This was usually asked in exasperation. It was then followed by a barely audible grumbled comment about Ava's mother having been the one to pack said box.

Most of the time it seemed to the girl as if her father had forgotten that she even existed. It was a lot more boring than she had anticipated. She had wanted to help her Daddy unpack. But there wasn't a lot she could do. Therefore, she spent a lot of the time playing with Floppy.

She moved haphazardly about the room making him jump from box to box and giving him a goofy voice. Daddy threw her occasional glances with a little grin as she did this, charmed by his daughter's imaginative play. Then he would go right back to unpacking and sorting.

They were more than an hour into it before Ava grew tired of occupying herself that way. She tucked Floppy under her arm and looked around at the first-floor hallway and the stacks of boxes and various unpacked pieces of furniture. None of it interested her much. It was all their same old stuff. What she was really interested in was exploring the new building they called home.

She surprised herself at how much the scary quality of the place had worn off. When they were first moving in, the place caused all sorts of anxiety in her. Now... Well, now it was like she belonged there. So, she wanted to get to know more about the place.

Her eyes drifted to the end of the hallway where the stairs resided, leading up to the second level. She'd been up there already and thought about detaching from Daddy's side to go up there and find Mommy. But she basically already knew what to expect up there. However, an entire wing of the ground floor level remained where she had spent no time investigating.

She cast a cautious glance at Daddy. He was bent over a box and his head and arms thrust inside it. He rummaged through its contents, grumbling about who knew what. She turned back to the hallway, staring that way for a bit.

She plucked Floppy out from under her arm and held the rabbit up in front of her. She gave the bunny a thoughtful look.

Ava knew Mommy and Daddy expected her to stay with one of them until they could look at the rest of the space together. But if she had Floppy with her, she wouldn't really be alone, would she? She gave her father one more look before deciding she could creep away and be back in a few minutes... probably without him knowing she was gone.

She turned to face Daddy's busy form and slowly started backing away. She was sure he would come out of the box, turn, and look directly at her. He would frown and in a stern voice ask, *Young lady, just where do you think you're going?* She would be filled with shame at having been caught and probably cry a little.

It was her only defense with him. It didn't work with Mommy that well. The little girl could never figure out why.

But Daddy didn't come out of his box. He continued to rummage in there even now that she was several yards away. She quickened her pace and turned around. She tip-toed, scurrying forward. She cast occasional worried glances over her shoulder. When she reached the point where the hallway bent and began the new wing of the old school, she halted. She turned back to her father who now appeared very small. He was out of the box now but still not looking her way. In both hands, he held what she thought was a picture frame. He studied it.

She watched him for another few seconds then darted around the corner.

She made it only a few steps before stopping again. Whereas the first hallway was well-lit with all the overhead lights turned on, the hallway stretching out before her was dim and grim. None of the banks of light were on and an unnaturally deep shadow lay over everything.

There was no ambient daylight filtering through the classrooms running along the side. The new industrial blinds her mother and father had installed before they moved in were doing their job.

Ava was having second thoughts about exploring this region of the school.

But she had come this far. Also, she felt an odd calmness about marching ahead. She lifted Floppy again and looked at him.

"I won't be afraid if you won't," she said to him.

The rabbit gave no reply. She didn't even pretend it had. She merely gave the stuffy a solemn nod and tucked him back under her arm. She took her next careful step into the dark hallway and then stopped and waited for something to happen. Nothing did. Then she took the next step, then the next.

As she progressed, she didn't feel encroached upon by the dark. Her eyes were already getting used to it.

She stopped when she came to the door of the first classroom of the wing. The door was closed and through the window in the steel door, she could it was thoroughly dark inside. She didn't feel at all well about checking out that room, so she moved on to the next.

A sudden sensation that she was no longer alone washed over her, and she stopped. Her skin went cold and goosebumps prickled her forearms. She was almost too afraid to turn around and look.

Almost.

She took two quick breaths and then suddenly spun to catch whoever it was that was staring at her. She expected to see her father following her, having realized she left his side and come looking for her. Instead, she saw only an empty hallway. She didn't even hear the approach of his footsteps.

He wasn't coming. No one was. She was alone.

Yet she couldn't shake the feeling that other eyes were on her.

She spun to face the other way. No one was there. Her attention felt pulled to the door she had just passed. The window. The solid black rectangle. If she went closer and peered inside, what would she see? It didn't matter because the window was too high up on the door for her to look through it.

But if she pulled the door open and looked inside…

No. She refused to do that. She was suddenly afraid of what she would see if she did.

She backed further into the hallway, keeping her eyes fixed on the door. She half-expected it to open of its own accord and someone hidden within the room to step out and reveal themselves. If that happened, she realized, she really would be trapped.

Whoever was hiding in there would stand between her and her Daddy down the other hallway. Then the mysterious person in that room could jump out, snatch her, take her away, and do whatever bad people did with the kids they stole.

Mommy and Daddy had warned her never to go anywhere with strangers or take anything a stranger offered if Mommy or Daddy were not around to say it was okay or politely decline.

The door remained closed. However, the feeling that she was not alone never diminished.

But Daddy had checked out the entire place last night, hadn't he? He said no one was hiding anywhere in their new home and they were safe. Then why did she feel this way?

Maybe it was what Mommy referred to as her overactive imagination. Maybe... but this didn't feel like her pretending and playing.

She continued to slowly back away from the door. She passed the door to the next classroom. She never bothered looking up at the rectangular window fixed in that door. She would never know what she would have seen if she had. What she would have seen if she had looked was a face that didn't belong.

But she would see it later.

She came at last to the end of the hallway and stopped. She felt far enough away from the first classroom that she could stop watching the door. Nothing and no one was going to come out after her. The problem was that she would have to go back that way.

She breathed a momentary sigh of relief, and her shoulders dropped a bit.

She turned her face to the side and saw another door. But it wasn't for a classroom. It was solid with no window. And instead of steel, it was composed of wood. Resting a third of the way down from the top was a word she didn't know. She squinted in the dark as she sought to read it. She was getting better at her letters and reading, though Daddy said she still had a long way to go before she was reading Dickens... whatever that meant.

She sounded out the word slowly, it feeling foreign in her mouth the entire time.

"Jan...i...tor. Jani...tor? Janit..."

"Ava!" came her father's resounding voice from nearby.

She nearly jumped out of her skin and a yelp escaped her as she spun to see him storming her way.

"What do you think you're doing, wandering off like that?"

She felt herself shrink as he approached.

"S...sorry, Daddy," she said, mustering the best cowed voice she could manage. It wasn't that hard considering the vulnerability she'd so recently felt passing the first classroom.

"Baby, we told you not to wander off! What if you'd gotten yourself stuck in a cabinet or something and we couldn't find you for a long time?"

Tears welled in her eyes – genuine ones, not the kind she sometimes worked up to get herself out of trouble. The day was young yet and she had already felt so much.

"I'm sorry, Daddy," she repeated as her shoulders shook.

He stopped and knelt before her. His stern expression turned to compassion, and he held his arms out to his sides. She gladly accepted the invitation and flung herself at him, wrapping her arms tight about his neck and squeezing until he pretended to be unable to breathe. Floppy was smooshed between them.

She drew away from him and smiled at the goofy face he made. Another tear or two still spilled down her cheeks but the worst of it was over. Daddy always seemed to make her feel better.

"Don't go running off like that again, okay? You had me worried there for a tick."

"Okay, Daddy," she replied, fully intending to obey him.

"Come on," he said, standing and picking her up. Let's get back to work, okay? Otherwise, you-know-who upstairs will have an aneurysm."

"A what?" Ava asked.

Daddy chuckled and said, "Never mind, sweetheart."

He turned and carried her back. They passed the nearest classroom, the window of which no longer sporting the face that Ava had missed the first time she had passed it. The other classroom, however, drew the girl's attention.

There was no face in that door's window either but in the swirling dark beyond it, Ava thought she detected the barest hint of movement. She gasped.

"What is it kiddo?" Daddy asked.

"It's..." and she trailed off since they were now moving passed the door. She almost raised her hand and pointed. Since she no longer felt the weight of that other presence, she did nothing. She shook her head and said, "I just don't like the dark down here."

"That's because the lights are turned off, silly," Daddy said. "We'll turn them on when we come and check out this space later today. It won't be so dark then. Good deal?"

"Good deal," she repeated, sounding entirely unconvinced. Her eyes drifted briefly to the retreating form of the door. It remained closed. Still, she couldn't shake the feeling that something was in that room. And she didn't like it.

11

Boy

Another night, another bad dream.

As Ava woke from this one, though, the nature of the nightmare fled from her. She possessed no memory of what it had been about. The only thing left for her was the terror.

But that was more than enough.

She rocketed to a sitting position, hugging herself. Fast, ragged breaths came, tearing through her chest like a football team breaking through a paper banner to storm out onto the field.

Her eyes darted about her room. This time she was not entirely bathed in darkness, though the hour was late. Her Daddy had installed a nightlight as a consolation, saying she was a big girl and needed to sleep in her own room. She couldn't keep coming into Mommy and Daddy's room every night just because she hadn't learned to be comfortable in her own space.

Did she try to argue the point? Of course, she did. But she was only six, so it made no difference. This time Daddy was holding firm; there was no way around it.

She relented and both parents accompanied her to her room and tucked her in. They spent several minutes with the girl, comforting and assuring her that all was well and she was completely safe in their new home. She had considered rehashing her experience of wandering from Daddy's side earlier that day but quickly clamped down on the idea. Bringing that up again might get her in trouble. Daddy hadn't told Mommy about it.

Ava was grateful as Mommy seemed more ready to pop with anger than usual lately.

When her parents had deemed that they had done all they needed to admonish the girl to remain in her room, they left. Daddy was the last one out. He paused at the doorway long enough to drop her a wink and smile, then he gently pulled the door closed.

Ava had fallen asleep despite her protests that she wasn't tired. Her parents had not stayed up much later themselves. It had been a long day filled with hard work. Progress had been made but there was a lot left to finish before either adult would comfortably say they were unpacked.

Ava had been out for about five hours when the dream had scared her awake.

Her eyes searched the room for any sign of danger. At the same time, her hands felt for Floppy. The rabbit was not on her bed.

The first thing she noticed was that her door stood open. Her tired brain, awash as it was in the chemicals of worry, worked to make sense of this.

Had Mommy or Daddy come back into her room to check on her? If so, why had they not closed the door when they left again? Unless...

Unless it was not Mommy or Daddy who came in.

And worse: unless whoever it was had never left.

Ava slowly turned her head to survey the rest of the room once more. Her head stopped moving as she came to the same corner of the room where she'd thought she'd seen someone standing and staring at her the night before. Her chest went cold as she gasped loudly.

Standing in that same corner was a young boy. In a flash of recognition, she saw that it was the same boy she had seen standing outside the front door of the old school. He gazed at her with the same wide, hyper-aware eyes as he had done before. It made Ava's skin crawl.

He had a dirty but pale face and dark, disheveled hair. He wore a light blue and white twill flannel shirt and jean overalls. His arms were hugged before him, clutching Floppy.

Jealousy stabbed at Ava's heart, momentarily interrupting the pervading fear she felt. The rabbit was hers and Mommy said that since it had cleaned up well enough that she could keep it. Now this boy had him.

She found her voice and shakily asked, "Who... who are you?"

Instead of answering, the boy jutted up an index finger and pressed it to his lips. Something clicked in the back of Ava's mind. That look he wore, that wide-eyed expression... it was fear. This boy was afraid of something.

She slowly shoved aside the covers and moved to get out of bed. But the boy urgently shook his head, still pressing his finger to his lips. She froze.

"What is it?" she whispered.

The boy only shook his head again, his face growing more worried. He held up a hand in a clear signal for her to stay put. A second later, his head jerked toward the door. He backed further into the corner, keeping his attention fixed on the doorway.

Ava followed his gaze, afraid of what she might see.

The door was only partially open, but it afforded more than a sliver of a view into the hallways. She watched that way for a long time but saw nothing. There was only the shadow-shrouded passageway. She was about to turn back to the boy when one of the shadows shifted.

It was barely perceptible, yet it was enough for Ava to catch it. Seeing it stabbed an icy spike into her heart, though she couldn't tell what it was.

The flesh of her cheeks and forehead felt heavy and tingly warm.

Her gaze shot back to the boy and found him cowering, pressed fully into the corner of the room and sinking lower. He jammed a thumb into his mouth and sucked it like he was a baby. Ava thought he looked to be about the same age as she was. He was maybe a little taller, but the way he hugged Floppy to him and the look of unadulterated fear on his face mirrored how she felt at that moment.

Her attention darted back to the doorway, not wanting to lose track of... well, whatever it was that was out there. At the same time, she didn't want to see it. She hoped in desperation that it would not come into her room.

The shadow in the hallway moved again. Now it came right to her door. It filled the space so that it was like looking into only blackness. Every little hair on Ava's body stood on end.

She was overpowered by the feeling that someone... no some-*thing*... was staring at her.

Now she couldn't help it. She sucked in a sharp breath and screamed.

STUDENT MISSING

THE FOLLOWING IS A SELECTION OF AN ARTICLE FROM THE CEDAR PARK HERALD, A LOCAL NEWSPAPER. DATED APRIL 11, 1987

Authorities reveal that a local student has gone missing.

Yesterday, after school let out for the weekend, students fled Cedar Park School, no doubt with plans for the weekend. One family, however, will not be relaxing as their young son failed to return home.

Patrick Reginald Harris, 8 years old, never made it home after school.

Sources indicate that the boy was reported missing around 8 p.m. last night. His family is reportedly frantic as it is highly unlike the individual in question to not return home immediately after school closes for the day. However, it is notable that his younger sister did make it home safely, having ridden the bus. Patrick is known to walk to and from school, therefore no witnesses aboard what would be his typical bus can confirm or deny his last known appearance.

No details are yet available regarding the circumstances that might have arisen to prevent the child from going straight home.

However, according to the chief of police, "Nothing is being ruled out as it is too early to determine anything of substance."

At this time, the family has requested any information be directed to the police.

12

SOMNAMBULISM

Daddy's response time was impressive. Not that it mattered. As soon as the scream erupted from her mouth, the shadowy form filling the doorway vanished. Seconds later, Daddy filled it with a look of pulse-pounding alarm stretching his face. He fumbled inside the door along the wall until his hand found the light switch. He flicked the light on, and the room was flooded with blinding brilliance that made both father and daughter wince.

"What is it?" he nearly shouted as his eyes fell upon his daughter. He wore only boxer shorts, revealing his softening form not yet touched by middle age.

Ava sat on her bed and looked back at Daddy, trying to come up with a way to explain the mad situation. She glanced at the boy for help, wondering what her Daddy would do when he realized a stranger was in their new home. But when her eyes came to the spot she had last seen him, the boy had vanished.

Floppy remained, sitting on top of the same boxes where he had been the night before.

Daddy tracked where she was looking and saw the rabbit. He mentally noted that the stuffy was not with his daughter unlike when her parents had put her to bed hours earlier. He cocked his head to one side and his brow drew down as he contemplated this. But then he shook his head in dismissal. He looked back at Ava and stood a little straighter, raising his eyebrows as he waited for an answer.

"There was a boy in my room. He had Floppy with him over there." She pointed to the corner where Floppy now sat, bent over to one side, his raggedy ears drooping down.

"A boy?" her Daddy asked with a note of disbelief in his words. His attention drifted back to the corner. He stared that way for a moment, then walked over there. He bent forward and glanced behind the stacks of boxes. He looked everywhere, even moving a stack aside and sliding back there. He poked around for a few seconds, then spun back to Floppy. He looked the rabbit up and down before snatching it from the stacked boxes. He held the stuffed animal up and gazed at it.

He held aloft the hand grasping the rabbit as he slid back into the unobstructed area of the room. He grunted as he approached Ava and held the rabbit out to her. She hesitated, then took Floppy from him.

"No boys back there," he casually observed. "Just boxes and clutter."

"There was a boy!" Ava insisted. "He was right there with Floppy. And... there was something else, too."

Daddy lowered himself to sit on her bed. He leaned forward to listen, but it was already becoming clear to Ava that this was nothing more than a kindness – a precursor to whatever it was

Daddy was already planning to say. But she would say what she had to, regardless. He had to know.

She leaned closer to the man and in a conspiratorial whisper, she said, "And there was a monster."

Daddy's lips went into a suddenly thin and tight line. His eyes took on a glint of something. It was the same look she'd seen on him when Mommy said something he found funny, but he didn't want to laugh out loud. So, he suppressed it.

"It's true!" she said, scrunching her face and jerking back in hurt.

He raised placating hands. "Okay, okay, Babe. I hear what you're saying. You saw something scary. I get it. But can I tell you something? It's something Daddy's and Mommy's know, and I think it's time to tell you. There are no monsters, kiddo. Monsters are just make-believe things for stories and movies and stuff. Okay? I think what happened is you had a bad dream and it seemed very real to you and it scared you. It scared you so bad that it woke you up and you screamed, thinking it was still happening."

"No, Daddy! I saw the boy and the monster *after* I woke up!"

"Dreams can be strange, Babe. They can feel like we're awake for them. Sometimes we can feel like we've woken up from a dream but really, we've just gone into another dream. I think that's what happened to you kiddo. Part of your cute little head was still asleep and still dreaming when you were waking up and you saw things that weren't really there." Daddy paused in thought, then said, "Can I ask you something?"

"Sure," Ava replied slowly and with great caution. She didn't like where this was going and was frustrated that her Daddy didn't believe her.

"Do you remember telling me you saw a boy outside earlier today? He was looking in at you through a window, right?"

"Yes, Daddy it was the same boy. He was right there in the corner, holding Floppy."

"I know it feels that way, Ava, but listen; it wasn't. It was just a dream. You probably dreamed about the boy because you saw him earlier and it startled you. Your funny little brain tucked away that experience and then trucked it out again when it was time to dream. That's all it was."

"Then why was Floppy over on the boxes instead of with me in my bed?" Ava asked. "I didn't get up and put him over there. The boy must have taken him."

Daddy drew a breath and pursed his lips. He narrowed his eyes as he gazed at her. He seemed to be weighing something. He blew his breath out in a noisy gust and said, "Okay, kid. I'm going to level with you. I'm going to tell you something about yourself that I don't think you know. Are you ready?"

"Ready?" she asked, her chest tightening, not liking where this was headed. "I guess so."

"Okay," he said, "here goes nothing. Ava, you are a sleepwalker."

She blinked in startled confusion. "A sleepwalker?" she repeated carefully.

"That's right," he said. "Sometimes you get up when you're asleep and you walk around. The first couple of times you did it, you scared the bejeezus out of your Mommy and me."

Ava sat dumbstruck by this revelation. She managed no response other than staring back at her father in utter shock.

He went on, "So, here's what I think happened last night and tonight. You sleepwalked over to those boxes and set your stuffy friend on top of them, then came back to bed. As you woke up, you dreamed you saw someone over there holding your rabbit and had a night terror. That's all it is, kiddo. Our brains do goofy and amazing things at night when we're asleep. So, you don't have to be afraid."

Ava found herself torn. She wanted to believe what her Daddy was saying, but it had all been too real. And she recalled that feeling she'd gotten when she was by herself for that brief time earlier that day.

"Can I come and sleep with you and Mommy again?" she asked. "Please?"

Daddy shook his head. "No can do, sweetheart," he replied. "You know you have to get used to sleeping in your new room. We've been over this. Now, do you want me to leave the night light on or do you want it off?"

"ON!" she shouted before he finished.

He chuckled, "Okay, okay. Just checking. Now it's way past time for bed. Let's get you snuggled back in."

He helped the girl back in and tucked her tightly into her sheets and covers. He made sure to stuff Floppy in beside her. It felt like she couldn't unwrap herself if she wanted to.

"Snug?" he asked.

In a breathy voice, she replied, "Very."

He grinned and headed for the door as he said, "Goodnight, sweety. Sleep tight."

Like she had a choice after how restrictive he'd made the covers.

"Night, Daddy. Love you."

"Love you, too, Baby." He blew her a kiss which she was too bound up to return. He winked at her, flicked off her light, and pulled the door closed.

As she lay in the dark, she periodically lifted her head and stared into the corner, expecting the boy to come out of hiding again. But he didn't show up again that night.

She had a hard time falling asleep again.

13

SEARCH

Days had passed since Ava saw the boy in her room. She was beginning to wonder if she had imagined him. Or maybe Daddy had been right, and it all really was just a dream.

Still, she stayed up late for the next several nights, expecting the boy to return. She also kept a wary eye on her door. What if it popped open in the middle of the night and something dark looked in on her again? Or worse, what if it came into her room?

Ava had no plan as to what she would do if any of these things happened. Mostly, she was just scared again. This creaky old school was not the happy place her parents had promised it would be.

At that moment, she toddled along after Daddy who was on a mission. A few important boxes were missing, and he was on the hunt for them. He surmised they must have simply been placed in the incorrect room.

He brought them to the junction on the first floor where the stairs led upward, and the other wing branched off at a different angle. He paused at the place where the two wings met and planted his fists on his hips as he stared down the empty hallway. All but one of the overhead lights were off. The one that remained live was twitchy, blinking on and off at random intervals. He reached up and scratched his chin.

"Something wrong at the panel?" he mumbled to himself.

Ava heard it though. She pressed close to the back of his right leg. She peered around him and gazed with trepidation at the dim path ahead. A little whimper escaped her.

Daddy glanced down at his little girl. "You okay, Pumpkin?"

Her eyes shot up to meet his. Floppy dangled at her side, clasped in a death grip. She tremblingly pulled the stuffed rabbit to her chest and squeezed it tight. She nodded but her father could read the trouble all over her.

He reached down and tousled her hair, giving her a lopsided grin. "Don't worry, Baby. I think there's just something funky with the electricity. We had the wiring checked and a new power panel installed before we moved in. Probably, there's just a loose connection or something."

She didn't understand a word of what he said, but the confidence with which he said it went a little way toward soothing her.

He added, "Maybe we'll see if your Daddy can't figure it out after we find the missing boxes. Okay?"

She nodded again, then turned to look back to the hallway with its sputtering light. Her unease returned in a rush. She didn't want to go down that way and she didn't want her Daddy to go either. It felt... dangerous. But she knew he was going to go and decided it would be better for him if she went too.

Daddy set off and Ava followed closely at his heels. A little too close.

"Ava, you're going to trip Daddy if you keep walking so close. Why don't you come around to my side, at least?"

She obediently came around and tried to keep pace with the man. All the while, she swept her gaze over her environment. She paid special attention to the steel doors of the two classrooms and the rectangular windows mounted in them. They were dark, like sharks' eyes that Ava had seen in a book once. Those black eyes had unsettled her when she first saw them. But they also fascinated her.

She asked her Daddy why their eyes were like that. He'd shrugged and said, "I don't know, Babe. I'm not exactly a marine biologist."

When she asked what that was, he chuckled and said, "Never mind kiddo."

Daddy strode up to the first door. That was the one she hated the most. That door and whatever stood behind it gave her the creeps. Her cheeks warmed and tingled as Daddy reached for the door. He twisted the knob and pushed... and nothing happened. The door remained fixed in place.

Daddy grunted and pushed again. Again, the door didn't budge.

He cast a curious look at his daughter and in a tone of disbelief said, "It's locked." He returned his attention to the door and dropped his right hand into his pants pocket. He fished around briefly, there was a jingling noise, and a moment later produced a ring thick with keys. "Good thing I brought this along."

He began thumbing through the keys, mumbling to himself. Ava watched with growing trepidation but hoped he didn't have a key to this room. Maybe they could leave it closed forever and whatever was in there would stay in there and never come out to bother anyone.

She had no idea what was in there, only that she didn't like whatever it was.

He tried several keys in the lock but none of them turned. As he neared the end of the keys, hope blossomed in Ava's chest. But then one of the keys turned in the lock and the door made a strange thudding noise. Daddy tilted his head slightly and adopted a questioning look. Then he shrugged and pushed the door open.

He stepped into the darkness, disappearing. Ava held her breath, not moving.

A heartbeat later the lights blinked sputteringly on in the room. Ava stepped forward and saw her Daddy standing inside the empty classroom, just off to the side. His hand was falling away from the light switches there. He reached the hand up and scratched the back of his head as he searched the space.

"Doesn't look like our missing boxes are in here," he grumbled.

A minor squeaking noise caught Ava's attention, and she jerked her head toward the corner of the room. There was a door there and she thought she witnessed minor movement, as if it were just closing.

"Daddy," she whispered. She never tore her eyes from the door but reached up with a fumbling hand until she found his arm and tugged on the sleeve.

"What is it, Ava?" he asked at normal volume, not sounding in the best of moods.

"That door," she whispered.

He tracked her gaze and saw what she was talking about.

"Yeah, what about it?"

"It moved," she continued to whisper.

"Probably just moved with the air current," he said. "We did just open the classroom door, so…"

"No," she hissed. "Someone's in there. I want to go, Daddy."

"No one is in there," Daddy said firmly. "I checked the whole place, remember?"

For the first time, Ava looked up at her father. Her eyes were pleading. But her mind was also working, maybe better than it ever had. She even surprised herself with the next thought that escaped her lips.

"Was this room locked before when you checked it?"

Daddy's mouth opened, he paused, then snapped closed again. "Well… no," he said. Under his breath, he added, "Weird." He turned back to the closet door and stared at it. He stepped toward it, but Ava tugged insistently at his sleeve again.

"Daddy, no!" The time for whispering was gone. It was a full-on whine now.

Her father pulled his sleeve from her grip, gave her an admonishing look, then said, "Chill out, kiddo. I'm just going to see what's in there. I mean, I doubt the movers would have shoved our missing boxes in there, but it's worth a look."

He favored her with one last look of resolve, then turned, and sauntered over to the door. It was not like the classroom doors, which were all made of metal. This one was comprised of old wood.

He slowly pulled it open. It groaned a terrible protest that sent a thousand slivers of ice into Ava's spine. She watched with mounting terror as Daddy stepped into the darkness beyond the door. She was too afraid to get near enough to see what happened to him.

There was an audible click and yellow light poured out of the empty doorway. Ava held her breath, waiting to hear her Daddy scream.

Instead, he popped his head out and said, "It's just an empty supply closet, kiddo. No monsters or bad guys hiding in here."

Ava took a step forward, then stopped. Then another. Then she burst into a little jog, covering the remaining distance in a hurry. She felt Floppy's legs bounce against her belly as she ran.

Daddy stood in a cramped closet and lifted his arm like a magician displaying a fine magic trick.

"See?" he said. "No big deal."

Ava stayed several paces away. Though the space appeared empty, just looking at it gave her a yucky feeling.

"Okay," she said sheepishly.

Daddy reached up to a thin pull chain dangling from an uncovered lightbulb. He tugged on it and the light went out. He stepped out, spun, and closed the door behind him.

"Alrighty," he said, "onto the next room."

They found the missing boxes in the second classroom, which had not been locked. Daddy seemed not to notice of this.

There were seven medium-sized to large boxes gathered in the center of the room. But both Daddy and Ava froze the instant they laid eyes on them. The boxes were open, and the contents were strewn about.

Daddy uttered a clear and nasty curse. He caught himself, gave his daughter an apologetic look, and said, "Don't tell Mommy I said that in front of you, okay?"

"Sure, Daddy," Ava said, still staring at the mess, entranced by it.

"Did the movers do this?" Daddy asked in disbelief. He shook his head as he reverently approached the disarray. "I can't believe they would do this."

The man's fists balled at his sides and his face darkened and he started talking to himself, as he normally did when he got upset. "I'm gonna call them and give them a piece of my mind. Demand a refund. This is unacceptable."

The longer Ava stared at the open boxes and haphazardly distributed items and gear, the surer she became of one thing: the movers had not done this.

She didn't even think they had placed the boxes in this room. She didn't know why she was sure of that, but she was.

This was someone – or some*thing* – else's doing.

14

Shopping

It wasn't often that Ava was allowed to sit in the front passenger seat of the car. She bounced with delight as she stared directly through the windshield. Well, almost directly. She was still fairly little and strained to see the street because the dashboard obstructed her view.

It was just her and Daddy. He told her that Mommy needed some space because she was stressing out over the special dinner party that they were going to be throwing in less than a week. He told her he needed to get some shopping done and was itching to get away from the new place and see their new town. Plus, he said with a knowing smirk, he wanted to get some daddy-daughter time with his little girl, and maybe if she did well during shopping, they could get some ice cream.

The promise of the treat was the cause of her glee. But also, she loved her Daddy very much and so enjoyed the times when it was just the two of them. She loved her Mommy, of course. There was no questioning that. But between her two parents, Daddy was the one less prone to snap or to lose his temper.

They pulled into the parking lot of a supermarket not far from their new home. It wasn't as big or nice as the one they had frequented when they lived in their old apartment. There also weren't very many cars.

Daddy parked the car, got out, and came around to Ava's side to let her out. Once she stood beside their car, Daddy took her hand and led her across the meager parking lot toward the store. She skipped at his side, humming a tune from one of her favorite shows.

They passed through the glass front doors – which were not automatic like the ones at the old grocery store where they used to shop. Just inside, there was a row of shopping carts nestled within one another. Daddy extracted one of these and unfolded the portion near the push bar for either a child to sit or for someone to store items that might get crushed by larger, heavier ones.

"Sit or walk?" Daddy asked, tossing a glance at Ava.

She made a thoughtful noise and tapped her chin. She said, "Sit!"

Daddy grabbed her under both arms, hoisted her into the air, and maneuvered her legs so they would slide through the two square openings. She was probably too big for it, but Daddy had a hard time accepting that she was no longer truly little. When she was in place she beamed up at her Daddy. He returned the smile and then they set off into the store.

He kept one hand on the push bar and fished the other into his pocket. A second later he withdrew his phone. He opened it, put in his pin, and then found the notes app where he'd made his shopping list. "Okay, looks like canned food is first," he said.

Ava made a face. "Not green beans," she said and let her tongue hang out in a sign of disgust.

"Not the canned ones, no," Daddy said. "Give me some credit, kiddo. I know you and I like the fresh ones best. We've still got a while, so I'm not getting stuff for Mommy's special dinner party yet. This time we're just getting normal…"

"Excuse me," interrupted a woman's voice from several yards away. Daddy turned to see who had called out and if it was his attention she was trying to get.

When his eyes fell on the woman he cursed.

"Daddy!" Ava reprimanded him.

He gave her a quick guilty look and said, "Sorry, pumpkin. It just slipped out."

The woman was now closer and waved her hand as she hurriedly approached Ava's daddy. Ava recognized her. The woman had come to their new home and talked to Mommy the day they moved in. She had been scary then and because of the look on her face, she was scary still. Ava shrank into her seat to the best of her ability.

Daddy turned around to meet the approaching woman and positioned himself between her and Ava.

"Excuse me," she said again as she stopped just outside of arm's reach.

"Yes, can I help you?" Daddy said in the cold, businesslike tone Ava had heard him use over the phone when dealing with someone trying to get Daddy or Mommy to do something they never would.

Sometimes you have to be firm with people, Daddy had said after he saw Ava staring at him after one such call had ended. *Otherwise, they'll just walk all over you and take what you don't intend to give.*

"You're the family that moved into the old school, aren't you?" the woman asked.

"Yes," Daddy replied crisply, "and you're the woman who accosted my wife and daughter on our first day in our new home, so be very careful what you say next."

The woman stiffened and her eyes widened at his directness.

"I'm trying to warn you," she said, regaining a bit of her composure. "That's not a good place. No one should live there."

"It's not so bad," Daddy replied. "It's working out for us so far. Why don't you let us worry about it? It's ours now."

"You don't understand…" the woman began but Daddy cut her off.

"No, I don't care. That's different. Go spread your crazy somewhere else. And don't bother us again." Daddy turned away from her and started pushing the cart away. But the woman scurried ahead and blocked their path. Her hands shot forward and took hold of the front of the cart.

"Please, you have to listen," she said. "You're not the first to have bought that place and it hasn't ended well for any of the previous owners."

"My line of credit is solid. And so is my lawyer. Get your hands off my cart."

"That's not what I'm talking about," the woman replied. "Check into it yourself at the library. Ask for news articles about the old school over the last thirty years. You'll see."

"Get your hands off my cart," Daddy repeated, a little more forcefully this time.

"Ask yourself," the woman said, ignoring his instruction, "why is it that after more than thirty years of disrepair and no one looking after the place is it in such good condition?"

"Guess they don't make them like they used to," Daddy said. Then, with his face going dark, he added, "Now, get your hands off my cart before I come over there and remove them myself. I will not be gentle."

The woman stared at him for a handful of heartbeats, removed her hands, and slid out of the way. But she wasn't done.

"As yourself why there are no bugs. No spiders. No mice have made their home in the abandoned school. Nothing sane that lives there stays sane for long... or *lives* for long."

For whatever reason, that brought Daddy up short. His face screwed up in thought as he seemed to consider the woman's words for the first time. Now that Ava came to think of it, she had seen no bugs or flies or anything like that at the new place. There were always little creepy crawly things that got into their old apartment. But not the new place. She had no clue what to make of that or why this strange woman should think it was a concern.

Daddy shrugged. "Who knows? Maybe it's some sort of weird natural phenomenon. Who cares? Now, if you don't mind, we've got some shopping to do." Daddy pushed past her but made sure to keep an unhurried pace to let her know he was not moved by her crazy interception.

"You need to listen to me," she called to his retreating back.

Daddy did not answer the woman. He just continued to push the cart away. Ava stared up at him with concerned eyes.

"Daddy?" she said.

"Don't you worry about her or what she said," he answered her unspoken question. "That chick is a kook, plain and simple. She's probably just lonely and trying to get attention."

"Okay, Daddy," Ava replied, not sounding as convinced as he would like.

He shifted his tone back to a happier one as he said, "Regardless of how the rest of our shopping trip goes, I think we've both earned some ice cream. Yeah?"

A wide smile cracked her face, and she bounced in her seat, forgetting all about the strange woman's words.

"What kind can I get?" she asked.

"After that? Whatever kind you want, Babe. Whatever kind you want."

15

Malfunction

The scream came from far away.

Ava's head jerked up and shot to the door to her room. It stood open and looked on the hallway bathed in late afternoon sunlight. In a flash, her heart was racing.

That sounded like Mommy.

She jumped off her bed and trundled to the door. She stuck her head out and looked toward the stairs. Mommy was supposed to be setting up her studio on the second floor. She stepped out of her room, her hands coming up from her sides to pick nervously at one another. She glanced back to her bed where Floppy sat. His body was slightly hunched over to one side and his long ears drooped, one of which covered his face.

She thought about retrieving him as she didn't want to go see what had caused Mommy to scream like that alone. But then she heard something behind her. She spun around to see Daddy coming her way from the cafeteria.

"Did you hear that, or did I imagine it?" he asked. His brow was dark and drawn down.

She nodded her head vigorously but said nothing. Daddy jogged forward but stopped when he reached his daughter. He gazed ahead at the stairs. His mouth worked like he was chewing on something.

At last, he said, "I better go see what the trouble is."

He lurched forward but a little whine from Ava stopped him. He turned and saw the worry etched on her features.

"What?" he almost snapped.

She took an involuntary step back from him. He immediately realized what he'd done and knelt to look the girl in the face. "Sorry kiddo, I'm just a bit testy after that lady at the store... well, never mind. I shouldn't have done that."

She stood still, hugging herself, still looking wounded.

Daddy reached both hands out to her, beckoning for her to come and receive a hug. She hesitated for just a fraction of a moment, then burst forward, throwing herself at him. He made an *oof* noise as she collided with him and wrapped her arms around him.

He pretended to choke and in a faux-strained voice said, "Take it easy, kiddo, you're gonna strangle me!"

She pulled back and smiled. "Silly Daddy."

"Silly Ava," he replied as he stood. He reached a hand down to her. She took it.

Before they set off to investigate what had caused the blood-curdling scream they had heard, Daddy paused and adopted a thoughtful expression. "You sure you want to come with me, Ava? If Mommy's really upset, then maybe it's not such a hot idea for you to goof around in her studio."

"I'm not going to goof!" Ava insisted.

"Okay," Daddy said with heavy resignation. "Fair warning has been given." He set off toward the stairs hand in hand with his daughter.

When they arrived at the second floor another scream pierced the air. Ava's shoulders jumped and she reconsidered whether she should have come. She could stop now, turn around, and go back to her room... but she didn't want to be alone on the first floor.

Even Daddy stopped in his tracks when the second scream happened. He stared in the direction of the open door down the hall, the one leading into Mommy's studio space.

"Everything okay?" he shouted timidly.

There was a long silence that followed. Daddy opened his mouth to call out again but stopped when Mommy appeared in the doorway. Even Daddy had to stop himself from retreating a step when he saw her.

She looked wild, almost unhinged. Her hair was crazy, and her eyes were laced with fury. Her lips split apart, and her teeth were partially exposed. Her shoulders rose and fell with her shallow but quick breaths.

"Do I look okay, Mike?"

"Well... not really, no," he replied.

"I'm not," she snapped. "I think my equipment must have been damaged during the move. And I swear, if I found out it was, heads will roll."

Daddy let go of Ava's hand and took a slow step forward. He raised both hands and said, "I hear you, Candace. I've got a bone or two to pick with them myself. But let me take a look at your setup and see if I can't figure out the problem, first, okay?"

She grunted loudly, spun, and disappeared back into her studio. Daddy and Ava traded apprehensive looks but then followed.

Daddy took a moment to scope the scene out, then said, "What seems to be the problem?"

"This crap doesn't work anymore. That a big enough problem?" She was seething.

Daddy raised his hands again in a placating gesture. "Okay, okay. Just trying to figure it out. I'm on your side."

"If you can figure it out, then by all means," she thundered. She folded her arms and leaned back against the table. "I've run through the entire setup procedure seven times, and I can't even get the system to turn on."

"That could be something as simple as a power cord, or…"

She interrupted, "Don't you think I thought of that? What kind of idiot do you take me for? I've switched out the cords with the spares each time."

"All right," Daddy said, his tone going slightly rigid. A look of challenge was beginning to form on his face. "I get that you're angry. But can you not take it out on me? I'm trying to troubleshoot for you. I'm not your enemy."

Mommy grumbled something under her breath and looked away.

"Close enough," Daddy said. He turned to look at the system. He bent over it, checking connections, the order in which everything was linked in the system, and a myriad of other things. He was no sound technician but he had picked up quite a lot just by virtue of helping his wife lug her equipment around to gigs and setting it up and tearing it down.

He came to a particular piece of gear and scratched his head as he looked at it. "Well, this is the logical place to start testing it," he said.

"I know," Mommy grumbled, her face sour. "I've tried it a gazillion times already, remember?"

He reached down and pressed a button. Lights blinked to life all over the system as the equipment came on. Daddy cast a look at Mommy and arched an eyebrow.

Mommy came away from the table and her arms dropped to her side as deep confusion took hold of her countenance.

"Wha... What did you do?" she stammered.

"I turned it on," he said.

"I... I tried that," she protested. "I tried that *a lot*."

"I don't know what to tell you," he replied, looking back at the gear. "It worked this time."

Mommy stood dumbfounded for a handful of heartbeats then collapsed in a heap on the floor. She began weeping uncontrollably.

Daddy and Ava exchanged startled looks. Ava just shrugged her shoulders and looked back at him helplessly.

Daddy darted to Mommy's side and knelt beside her the way he had done with Ava not long before.

"Hey, take it easy," he said. "It's okay. It works now."

"How?" she sobbed.

He gave her a wide grin, spread his arms out to the sides, and said, "I just have the magic touch."

That didn't seem to help. She fell forward, her shoulders heaving as she wailed. He reached out a hand and rubbed her back. She didn't appear to notice. She just kept on unraveling.

After a few minutes of this, she straightened again. She was still weepy, but the worst of the storm appeared to have passed.

"I don't need this right now," she said. "Everything has to be perfect."

Comprehension dawned on Daddy's face.

"Is that what this is about?" he said, grinning. "Oh, honey, they're going to love you."

"No!" she insisted. "It has to be just right, or I'll never break through. I'll be stuck as a small, no-account local musician with aspirations headed absolutely nowhere. And my mom will have been right. I can't have that."

"Hey," he said, his tone going from fun-long to deeply serious in a heartbeat, "that's enough of that talk. Your mom isn't here and even if she were, her opinion has no bearing on your success. Do you hear me? None. She can take her garbage opinion and go shove it where the Sun don't shine as far as I'm concerned."

More sniffles from Mommy, but at least she was calming down.

She said, "I don't know, Mike. Maybe we should call the dinner off."

"I think that's a bad idea, Candace," he said. "Listen, you've got this. Your studio is up and working. You've got finished tracks to share and they're great. I mean really great, okay? Ten-to-one odds say they'll have a contract drawn up in the next few days after the dinner."

"I don't even have an agent," she said.

"You don't need one," he replied. "You've got me, and I'm better than an agent. I play hardball with the best of them."

Mommy seemed to notice Ava for the first time. The two of them locked eyes. Something danced on Mommy's face, but Ava couldn't read it for the life of her. It felt like a staring contest that lasted forever.

At last, Mommy said, "Where's your friend?"

"My... friend?" For the briefest of desperate moments, Ava thought she was talking about the boy she had seen in her room late at night a few days ago.

"Yes. I haven't seen you without that ratty old thing since you found him."

"Floppy!" Ava said, remembering that she had neglected to retrieve the stuffy before she and Daddy had set off to investigate the scream Mommy had made. "He's in my room on my bed."

"Why don't you go play with Floppy, kiddo? Mommy and Daddy have to talk about some stuff. Run along now."

Ava hesitated and looked at Daddy. He gave her a simple nod. He glanced back at Mommy one more time but found her to be a stone wall. Nothing was getting through in either direction.

"Okay Mommy," she said. She turned and left. She came to the stairs and stopped. She didn't want to go back to the ground floor by herself. But she knew that if she waited, she might get in trouble for disobeying Mommy. She tossed a final look over her shoulder. Mommy or Daddy must have closed the door to the studio.

She turned back to the stairs and carefully made her way down them, ever listening for the sounds of someone or something that didn't belong moving around. She was met by utter silence... which might have been worse.

16

SHADOW

Ava trundled down the stairs. She was caught up in her worry about Mommy and Daddy. But especially Mommy. Sometimes she got like this, and it took Daddy a long time to help her. But Ava had never quite seen her mother as manic as she just had.

When she reached the bottom of the stairs, she stopped. Her eyes drifted to her left, to the unoccupied wing of the ground floor. A single light flickered with half-life toward the end of the hallway. The battle between the winking light and the pervading darkness unsettled her even more than she already had been.

But more than that, something was wrong with the scene. Her gaze went to the first classroom door halfway down the hall. It stood open.

That was not how Daddy had left it.

Ava's little heart began to race. She shivered and lifted her hands to rub her arms. It was then that she realized she was without her special new friend, Floppy. She briefly considered rushing back up the stairs and trying to get back into the studio where Mommy and Daddy were doubtless already fighting. But she knew from experience that would not serve her. Not only would she be repelled by her Daddy, but the man would also sternly scold her.

She could simply wait outside the door for them to finish but she understood this would only delay the same effect. It might even be worse. Both would be pretty mad if they knew she had waited just beyond the door and listened to their muffled fight.

That meant she could only continue and do her best to avoid the scary room in the disused part of the old school. She watched the dim path a little longer then turned to head toward her room. She took a step, then faltered. She stopped again.

She had left the door to her room open, and it still was. But she was certain she had seen the barest hint of motion upon turning toward it. It was like catching the tail end of someone ducking through the door.

There hadn't been enough to discern any information other than the movement itself. She wasn't altogether certain she had truly seen anything. But she wasn't about to take any chances, either.

Ava turned to head back up the stairs and intended to pound on the studio door until they let her in. This progress was immediately impeded when she noticed what appeared to be an unnaturally shaped shadow standing at the top of the stairs. The strangest thing about it was that it seemed unattached to anything physical. It merely floated in the air.

She was suddenly overcome by a sense that she was being watched, even though the shape had no discernible eyes. The fear threatened to suffocate her.

She took a cautious step backward, never tearing her eyes from the creepy shadowy figure. The thing didn't move to follow her, at least not yet. She stepped back again.

She was now steadily backing toward her door. She chanced a look in the direction of her door. There was nothing unusual she could see yet. However, she couldn't see much of her room through the slivered opening of the door. There was plenty of space for someone to hide.

When she glanced back to the shadow she gasped. The dark form had come a third of the way down the steps in the brief time she had looked away from it. A yelp of surprise escaped the girl. She wouldn't make the mistake of taking her attention off it again.

Thankfully, now that she was staring at the thing again it seemed to have ceased its pursuit. She hoped that meant it wouldn't move as long as she was watching it. That appeared to be holding true thus far. She refused to look away – even if ever-so-briefly – to test it, though.

The question was, where she should go? Her original plan had been to return to her room to retrieve Floppy. Then she likely would have stayed put and waited for Mommy and Daddy to finish their unpleasant business. By then it would have been around dinner time and maybe Ava could talk her parents into letting her watch a movie.

All of those plans were out the window now. She didn't know that if she made it to the haven of her room whether or not closing the door would keep the thing out. She couldn't lock the door.

Daddy had seen to it that she could not accidentally trap herself in her room.

She inched closer to the open door. Without looking it was hard to tell if her unseeing aim was adequate.

Her back came up against something solid and cold. It was the steel doorframe. She slipped inside, stretching her neck to watch the shadowy figure. That's when her theory about it never moving if it was watched collapsed.

Before her head disappeared through the door, the thing came rapidly the rest of the way down the stairs and made a B-line for her. The speed at which it crossed the distance caused her heart to leap into her throat.

Ava jumped back while grabbing for the door at the same time. She tugged at it with all her strength and flung it closed. The last thing she saw before the door slammed into place was the tall shadowy form looming in front of her.

She backed away from the door, expecting it to burst back open and for the dark thing on the other side to come rushing in to get her. She would have screamed but she couldn't seem to catch her breath well enough to do so.

She continued to scurry away from the door until her legs bumped into her bed. She dropped involuntarily onto the bed and thrashed about at the surprise of falling. She scrambled and fell off the other side of the bed. When she landed on the floor, she realized she could no longer see the door. She shot up and stared at it.

It remained closed and there was no sign that anything was trying to get in. But she wasn't ready to feel relieved yet. Her little chest heaved as her breaths came in ragged, shallow gasps.

After several moments when the door stayed closed, she allowed herself to feel a little bit safe. She dropped her eyes to the bed to locate Floppy.

But the rabbit was nowhere to be seen. Her eyes shot to the floor immediately around her feet, guessing she had knocked him off the bed in her mad scramble across it. However, the stuffed critter was not on the floor either.

With her confused face pointed downward at the area around her feet a new sensation crawled up her spine and caused her scalp to tingle. In that breathless instant, she knew she was not alone.

She lifted her face and slowly turned it to the corner of the room, the one where she had seen the boy a few nights earlier.

And there he stood, clutching Floppy, and staring at her with those hyper-wide eyes.

School Suspended Following Tragedy

The following is a selection of an article from the Cedar Park Herald, a local newspaper. Dated April 13, 1987

Cedar Park Township has been rocked by tragedy.

Patrick Reginald Harris, the young missing local student has been found. His body was discovered Monday morning in a locked supply closet at the Cedar Park School.

He appears to have been brutalized, bound, and abandoned for dead by an unknown individual or perhaps multiple assailants.

Considering the nature in which his body has been recovered, a murder investigation has been opened.

Police request that the family's privacy be respected at this time.

17

Patrick

She almost stumbled backward over her bed again when she saw him. He made no threatening move. Instead, he appeared to cower in the corner.

She glanced at the door to make sure the dark thing beyond hadn't taken the opportunity of her distraction to slip in. The heavy steel door hadn't budged and there was still no signal that any change in this was in the offing.

Relaxing infinitesimally, she regarded the boy once more. He continued frozenly gazing back at her. Now it was just a question of who would break the tension.

"Who are you?" Ava asked.

The boy did not reply. Instead, he darted his face toward the door, focused on it for a while, then returned his attention to Ava. He pulled the stuffed rabbit closer to his face as if that could obscure his presence.

"It's okay," Ava said. She tucked her lower lip between her front teeth and thought for a second about what to say next. Then she said, "I'm not going to be mad. But why did you take my rabbit?"

"Your rabbit?" the boy said in a meek voice. He tightened his hold on Floppy. "He's *my* rabbit. Why did *you* steal him?"

Ava blinked and her head drew back a little. "I... I didn't steal him. I found him. My Mommy cleaned him up for me and said I could keep him."

"Well, he's mine," the boy said unhappily. "He's been mine for a very long time."

A jealous and protective urge arose in Ava. It wasn't quite anger. Not yet at least. She didn't realize it, but Ava was sometimes prone to fits of mood swings like her Mommy was. One was steadily building at the moment, but it was only at the beginning stages.

She took a deep breath. She asked, "Why did you leave him in our new home?"

The boy's head tilted to one side and his face clouded with confusion. "Home? What do you mean? This is a school."

"It's not a school anymore," Ava said. "Mommy and Daddy bought it so we can change it to a place for us to live and a studio for Mommy to work."

The boy's countenance changed again. His eyes widened once more, and his jaw dropped. "You can't live here," he said flatly. "You have to go."

Ava's emotional temperature ratcheted up another notch. "But... we bought it. Daddy says it's ours. We don't have anywhere else to go. Our old apartment is for someone else, now. That's what Mommy said."

"You can't stay," the boy repeated.

"Why not?" Ava said, ready to throw her hands up. Exasperation was now leaking into her voice. Her belly was warming, and the sensation was climbing. It would soon reach her chest, and then her head. When it got to her eyes, then it would turn into trouble.

"Because," the boy replied as if the answer were obvious, "this is where *I* live." He paused, leaned forward, and spoke once more. This time, however, the meek, broken nature of his tone had changed, and the words came out with authority. "And I'm not alone here."

Ava thought about the dark and shadowy shape that had pursued her to her room. She didn't think there was anything that she could do about that thing. Mommy and Daddy would have to figure out how to get rid of it. But she was confident she could explain to the boy that he couldn't live in the old school any longer. He would have to find another place.

Yet she wondered about that. Where had he been hiding for the past several days that her family had lived there? How had Daddy missed him on his search through the place? Maybe he knew of some secret spaces to tuck himself into when her family was around.

It didn't matter. He would have to leave. The school was theirs now. Mommy and Daddy had saved for years to buy it.

"This is our home now," Ava said with confidence. "You can't hide in here anymore."

"Hide?" he barked a mirthless laugh. He slowly lowered Floppy away from his chest and now the stuffed rabbit dangled at the boy's side in one hand. He was short – shorter than Ava by an inch, though Mommy always said she took after Daddy's side and his family were all tall people. His skin was pale and dirty. His hair looked like it hadn't been washed or combed in ages.

"I'm not hiding here," he added. "I go wherever I want whenever I want in this school. It's my place and I know every inch of it. I've been here a long time. You are the strangers here, coming in where you're not welcome! None of the strangers last long." He shook his head slowly from side to side. "Besides," he said, "the other one doesn't want you here either."

A sudden spike of concern was driven into Ava's heart. Her face jerked toward the door again. She was sure she would find it open and the dark shadowy thing lunging for her. But the door remained closed and no one and nothing else had entered her room.

Her room. She must never forget that Mommy and Daddy promised her she was going to have a room all to herself. And this funny little boy was not going to take that away from her.

"No," Ava said, feeling the rising bodily warmth just about reach her eyes. She knew the eruption was almost upon her. She hated the experience as it always left her feeling yucky afterward. But she had also discovered something else about the episodes. Something useful.

When it got bad enough for her to explode in uncontrolled anger, sometimes the adults sought ways to assuage her, to placate the wrath pouring from her. She didn't think of it in these terms, of course. To her, it meant she sometimes got what she wanted when she lost control of her emotions.

She disliked going about it that way, and she could never fake it well enough to get by. No, it had to be genuine before others sympathized with her.

If she erupted with emotion now, maybe the boy would see how useless it was to argue and would give in. She was almost there.

"Besides," he said, "I couldn't leave even if I wanted to."

What was this? There was a sorrow in the boy's face and words that gave Ava pause.

"What do you mean?" she asked, still feeling the warmth and rage built up just below the surface.

"I'm stuck here," he said. He lifted Floppy to his chest again and squeezed him. "I died here a long time ago and I've never been able to leave the school."

Ava blinked in startlement. "Died?" she said. "You're standing right here, aren't you?"

He buried his face in the back of Floppy's head and soft sobbing sounds came from him.

"No," he said. "I think I'm a ghost."

Ava gasped and took an involuntary step backward. She couldn't believe it. She realized then that she didn't know very much about ghosts. Mostly what she knew was from cartoons. She doubted those were of much help.

Her mind swirled like a tornado as she considered her situation. And his.

Finally, after a long uncomfortable pause, she stepped closer to the boy and said, "My name is Ava. What's yours?"

The boy ghost sniffled as he lifted his head from the stuffed rabbit. He looked at her with hope in his eyes.

"Patrick," he said.

18

JOE

"How did you die?" Ava asked with awe in her voice. She'd never met a dead person before. And she never expected to be able to talk with one if she ever did. Based on the TV shows and movies she'd seen, dead people mostly just sort of lay there in a coffin and never do much of anything.

Patrick narrowed his eyes slightly as he watched her. She hoped she didn't make him mad by asking. She was genuinely curious.

"This was my school a long time ago. After what happened to me and a little bit after... that's when they closed it down."

"How long ago was it?" Ava asked.

He squeezed his eyes closed and thought. "I don't know," he said. "I was seven when I died. I wasn't very good at telling the time back then. But... it's harder now. Everything is different after you die."

Ava lifted a hand and scratched the back of her head in a perfect replication of her father. "I don't understand," she said.

"I don't either," Patrick replied. "I've been a ghost a long time. Much longer than I was ever alive, I think. Do you know how long the school has been closed?"

She shook her head. "Sorry," she answered. "I'm not very good at time, either."

He absently nodded. "Okay," he whispered, his hopes of finding some kind of answer about himself dashed. It made Ava sad to see him like that.

"Maybe I can find out," she blurted. "I can ask my Mommy and Daddy. They'll probably know."

Patrick's eyes brightened a little. "Yeah?"

Ava smile. "Sure," she chirped.

The two of them fell quiet as they watched one another. Finally, Patrick spoke up again.

He said, "It was a Friday. The last day of school for the week. All of us kids loved Fridays because once school was out, we could go outside and play all weekend."

Ava scrunched up her face. She didn't like playing outside very much. She preferred to stay inside and mess around on her tablet, play games with Daddy, or listen to Mommy make music.

Patrick continued, "But I liked Friday for a different reason. It meant I could get away from the mean boys."

"Mean boys," Ava repeated in a whisper.

Patrick nodded again. "Yeah. The worst one was Joe. He picked on me and my sister. But especially me. He was older than I was and tall. And strong. He'd push me down. He'd take my things or knock my books out of my hands. He'd rip my clothes. Sometimes, he'd just beat me up."

"I don't like mean people," Ava said. But she wasn't thinking of other kids she'd known. She was thinking about her grandma.

Her Mommy's mom. Ava only met her a few times that she could remember, but she hated every one of them. She always said mean things about Mommy and Daddy. She never came right out and said mean things about Ava... but the way the old woman looked at her was enough.

Patrick's eyes were far away as he continued. "Sometimes my dad would catch them hurting me or my sister, Maggie, and he'd run them off. My dad worked here as a janitor. I asked my dad once why he wouldn't beat them up in return, so they'd stop. He said he would but then he would lose his job and then we'd be out on the street. Joe's dad was on the school board and my dad said he was mean, too. And he had a lot of friends in town. My dad wouldn't be able to find a job anywhere."

The boy fell quiet, and Ava got the impression that he hesitated to go on. He looked at her and she gave him a weak smile. He returned it, then he pressed forward.

"On that Friday, I brought my stuffed rabbit for show-and-tell. I brought him because he was the only toy I had and my most favorite thing in the world. When Joe and his friends saw me carrying him to school, they rode their bikes up and blocked the sidewalk." A shudder ran through Patrick as he recalled the chain of events.

"They were much bigger than me. And they were a few years older. Joe was fourteen. They laughed at me and made fun of me and my 'baby toy.' Joe got off his bike and came up to me. I was so scared. He snatched my rabbit away and held it high above my head. He kept telling me to take it away from him but every time

I got close and jumped to try and reach, Joe would slap me. I cried and Joe and his friends laughed more."

Patrick paused as his face darkened. He said, "Joe took out a knife, a switchblade. He pushed a button and the blade came out. He stabbed my rabbit in the back and started to tear a hole in the back. I was sitting on the ground, my face still hurting from one of his slaps. But when I saw him tearing up my rabbit with his knife I got back up. I was mad. I ran at Joe as fast as I could and crashed into him, knocking him over. He tripped over his bike, fell, and his head hit the sidewalk. He got knocked out but there was blood, too. A lot of blood. His friends just stopped and stared at me. I reached for my rabbit, snatched him up, and ran away. None of the other boys chased me. I couldn't believe I had gotten away."

"Was... was he hurt bad?" Ava asked.

Patrick shook his head gravely. "No," he said. "He still made it to school. He had a big white bandage on his head and when he looked at me it scared me. I saw he was really angry. I knew if I wasn't careful, he was going to beat me up bad this time. I did my best to stay away from him, but I knew he was trying to get me. I tried to stay close to my dad. I told him what happened and that I was scared Joe was going to get me. Dad told me to do my best to keep away from Joe but he couldn't have me hanging at his side all day. He had work to do. Everything was okay and I kept away from Joe almost the whole day... until school was out, that is."

"What happened?" Ava asked with a sinking feeling.

"After the last bell, I couldn't find my dad or my sister. Sometimes she got sick, and Dad would have to take her to the hospital.

I think that must be what happened, but I never found out. Joe found me first. He grabbed me and hauled me into an empty classroom and closed the door. He put his friends outside to keep people out while he hurt me."

Patrick paused again and stared at Ava. His eyes were grim, and his mouth was a thin, dissatisfied line. He went on, "He clamped his hand over my mouth and nose so hard I could barely breathe. Then he punched me in the stomach. His hand on my mouth kept me from screaming and being heard by a teacher. He hit me a few more times until I couldn't stand anymore. I lay on the ground, moaning. I couldn't see very well. Everything seemed to be covered in a thin black cloth swirling with dancing stars."

Another shudder ran through Patrick. Ava found the boy's story repulsive yet at the same time she had to know what happened next.

"He picked up my rabbit and shoved it in my face. I was too weak to take it from him. And when I tried, he would kick me. 'How do you like fighting back, now, huh, kid?' he said to me. 'What are you gonna do this time? You gonna tell your daddy?' Joe looked around until his eyes landed on the closet in the corner of the room. He grabbed the back of my shirt collar and dragged me into the closet. I tried to get free but then he'd just hit me again and again until I stopped. Inside the closet, he tore strips out of my shirt and tied my hands and my ankles. Then he took off one of his shoes and then peeled the nasty sock off his foot. He shoved it into my mouth. I tried to spit it out, but he took his other sock and tied it around my head, like a gag. It tasted awful. It was... it was the last taste I ever had in my mouth. He stood over me and kicked me in the belly one last time. He then turned off the light in the closet, stepped out of it, and closed the door, leaving me in the dark. I fainted. No one came to check the closet before the school was closed and locked for the weekend. I died in that closet, slowly. I wasn't found until school the following Monday morning."

"That's so sad," Ava said.

"I'm not done," Patrick said, his eyes fierce and his voice grim.

19

Revenge

"What about the monster?" Ava asked abruptly. Patrick wasn't disturbed by the interruption. He merely nodded his head in a single solemn gesture.

"That's what I meant when I said I wasn't finished," he replied. "But... how do you know about him?"

"He chased me," Ava answered.

Now Patrick's ghostly mouth dropped open in astonishment.

"He chased you?" he repeated. "You saw him and everything?"

"Just before I came in here," she said. "I was coming down the stairs and I saw it watching me. When I got to the bottom of the stairs, it came after me, so I ran in here. What is it?"

"Not 'what'," Patrick said with a pained look. "But 'who'. It's Joe. He's another ghost like me."

Ava blinked a few times, astonished. She didn't know what to say, mostly because she didn't understand. Patrick read her confusion and supplied an answer.

"My dad is the one who found me," he began as yet another shudder ran through him. "He was unlocking the school on Monday morning. He was the only janitor the school could afford and very few others had keys. And no one offered to do it for him, even though I was still missing, and he was a terrible mess. But finding me pushed him over the edge.

"When the first students arrived, they were all kept outside. The police came and took my body away and spent hours here, investigating. There was no school that day. But I was still here. I watched the whole thing all day, trying to get someone's attention. But no one ever saw me. Well, almost no one.

"It didn't take long for the news to spread among the kids waiting around that morning to be sent home. A kid had been found dead in the school. By then everyone knew I had gone missing, so it wasn't hard to figure out whose body they had found."

Patrick stopped and looked away as if he heard something. Ava hadn't heard anything, however.

"What is it?" she asked.

"Bells," he replied absently.

"Bells?" she asked.

He turned his face back to her. He looked scared. "Yes," he said. "I hear them once every day. I have since the day I died. It means the collector is close.

"The collector?" she asked.

"That's what I call him. He's a scary-looking man in a black robe who walks up and down the street once a day, ringing his bell. He uses it to call the dead, like me. I think he's supposed to collect us, and we go with him somewhere else. But he scares me, and I don't want to go with him. So, I stay away from him."

Ava slowly nodded with awe as a creeping sensation crawled over her heart.

The two of them were silent for a while. Patrick at last tore his focus off some undetermined point in the distance and said, "There. He's gone now. Where was I?"

"You said one of the students saw you," she supplied.

"Right," Patrick said. "That was Joe. It happened while they were carrying my body out of the school. It was lying on a stretcher and wrapped in a big black bag. The students had been chattering away until that moment. Then they all fell dead quiet. I was watching from the front doorway. They brought my body right past me. But I wasn't paying attention to it. I was staring at Joe. He and his friends were among the gathered students. All of them but Joe was watching my body be carried to an ambulance. Joe on the other hand was staring right at me.

"He was white as a sheet and trembling. His friends didn't bother asking what was wrong. I guess they thought they knew. They had all been in on what happened to me. Yet none of them but Joe could see me. I have no idea why. I stared right back at him.

"Not long after that, most of the kids were dismissed. My dad saw to it that the police questioned Joe and his friends. I think he knew they were responsible. But then Joe's dad showed up with another man. He was dressed in a nice suit and started barking at the police about questioning his clients without their lawyers present. He then asked if the boys were under arrest. The police officer hemmed and hawed about this but ultimately said 'No.' He hurried to add that they would need to be questioned at the station later that day. The man in the suit accepted this, then turned to Joe and his friends and told them to come with him. The police let them go and my dad was beside himself."

"They weren't caught?" Ava asked, the words sounding sour.

"Not by the police," Patrick said. "But that doesn't mean Joe got away with it. Like I said, I'm sure my dad knew who was responsible."

A sinking feeling filled Ava's gut. "What did your dad do?"

"I couldn't leave the school, so I don't know most of it. I have no idea how my dad got his hands on Joe, but in the middle of the night a few days after I was found my dad came back to the school, dragging Joe's unconscious body. The side of his head was bloody, his hands and feet were tied, and he moaned every once in a while, so I knew he was still alive.

"He brought Joe to the same closet where I had been found. He stood over Joe for a long time, just glaring down at him. He started kicking him until Joe woke up again. Joe was confused about where he was and what was happening to him. He kept screaming for my dad to stop. My dad said, 'Did you stop for my boy?' Joe looked at him and only then realized who was attacking him.

"He started to scream for help. After a few more hard kicks, my dad bent down, grabbed Joe by the shirt, and pulled him up so they stared at each other's faces. My dad was furious, and Joe was terrified. He said, 'No one is going to help you ever again.' He slammed Joe against the wall. His head hit hard, and his eyes rolled up white. My dad was a big man, and strong. And even though Joe was much bigger than me, he was still just a kid and no match for my dad. I stood there watching the whole thing."

Ava barely managed to squeak out, "Is that... is that when Joe died? When your dad hit his head?"

"No," Patrick said. "He fell to the floor moaning and then he threw up. My dad said, 'You stupid kids are always making the janitor clean up after your messes. Now look at you. *You're* the mess. And it's time to finish the job. And I'm going to do it in the same place you killed my boy.' There was so much hate in his eyes. It was like a house fire that had gotten out of control. There was no stopping him even if I wanted to. But..." Patrick trailed off and his eyes squinted. His face turned dark, and it sent a chill down Ava's back. He finished in a whisper, "...but I didn't want him to."

Ava gasped. Patrick flashed a look at her that made her pull back. He growled, "Joe murdered me and got away with it. How would you feel if that happened to you? Or your Mommy and Daddy?"

Ava drew back like she had been slapped. Patrick stared at her with a reprimand in his expression but said nothing else about it. Instead, he continued his story.

"My dad left the closet for what felt like forever. I thought he was going to leave Joe to die like Joe did to me. But a while later, he returned with steel rods and a rope. The steel rods belonged to a disassembled heavy-duty frame the school used to sometimes hang big banners and posters. It had been donated by Joe's dad.

"Joe continued to writhe and groan on the floor of the closet. Dad ignored this as he rigged up the frame. As he did so, he started talking to Joe. It wasn't mean like before though. It was casual-like and that somehow made it worse. He said, 'Recognize this, Joe? Your dad bought it. Just like he bought you a lawyer. Just like he bought everyone in town whose opinion matters. That's why we have to do it this way, Joe. Because your dad bought your way out of trouble. How many times has he done that, I wonder? Well, not anymore. Whatever he did to get you and your friends off the hook, well, that was the last time. He thinks he's so much better than everyone else because he can buy whatever he wants, including getting his punk son out of jail. I could never buy even a quarter of the things he buys. Not even a tenth. I certainly can't buy back the life of my boy. And now your dad gets to know how it feels to not be able to buy his way out of something. He'll know how it feels to be like me. Won't that be a kick?'

"Joe whimpered on the ground. He begged my dad to let him go. He promised he wouldn't tell anyone what the man had done. He promised my dad he wouldn't be punished. My dad just chuckled. He said, 'Do you think I care about that? They can throw me behind bars, or they can fry me in the electric chair for all I care. All I want is your blood. Don't you get that, yet?' My dad shook his head and laughed again as he finished rigging up the frame. He'd already tied the rope into a noose and casually slung part of it over the top bar of the frame. He reached down and dragged Joe back to his feet. He held him in place, staring at him with cold, dead eyes. He nodded then reached up with one hand and grabbed the noose. He pulled it down and looped it over Joe's head. Joe begged again. In a cold voice, my dad asked, 'Did you have mercy on my boy?' Joe had no answer. My dad said, 'Right.'

"My dad walked around the other side of the frame. Just then Joe tried to make a run for it. The closet door had been left open and Joe bolted for it. But my dad was quick. He snatched the rope and yanked hard. Joe's feet flew into the air, and he landed hard on his back. He moaned and rocked back and forth. My dad started pulling on the rope, dragging Joe back toward the frame. Joe tried to get his feet under him but every time my dad pulled, the kid lost his footing and crumpled to the floor again. When Joe was even with the upright part of the frame my dad pulled slowly and Joe's feet left the ground for the last time while he was alive.

"My dad said, 'How do you like it when someone much bigger and stronger than you picks on you? Oh, and by the way; I have nothing to tie this rope to, so if you don't mind, I'll just hold onto it myself until we're finished. Okay?' By then Joe was kicking his feet and fighting to breathe. It took a long time for him to die. My dad was exhausted when it was over. He dropped the rope, and Joe fell in a heap on the floor. My dad checked for a pulse just in case, nodded, then walked out of the closet. That was the last time I ever saw my dad. Joe's body was found the next day. The school closed after that. But that wasn't the last time that I saw Joe. The first time I saw that shadow following me, I knew it was him. He stuck around like I did. He wants to catch me and take his revenge."

"Can he hurt you? You're both..." she trailed off, not wanting to say that they were both dead. Instead, she finished, "You're both ghosts."

"I don't know for sure, but I don't want to give him the chance. I can move things in the living world, maybe he can hurt me in the world of the dead." Patrick still held Floppy but now he merely dangled at the ghost boy's side. Ava's eyes flicked to the stuffed rabbit then back to Patrick. Patrick noticed.

He looked down at the toy for a long time, then held him out to Ava.

"Here," he said. "You take him."

Ava, startled by the offer, said, "Are you sure? He was your special friend."

"Toys aren't really our friends, Ava. They're just things. But maybe…" he hesitated and bit his lower lip. "Maybe *I* could be your friend?"

Ava nodded. "Yeah," she whispered.

"But you can't tell your mom and dad about me, okay? They'll think you're crazy and make you see doctors or something."

"Oh," she said with a hint of surprise. "Okay, I guess."

She reached a cautious arm forward and grabbed Floppy. Patrick held the rabbit a moment longer before letting go. Ava quickly drew the stuffed treasure to her heart.

"Since we're friends now," Patrick said, "maybe you can help me stay away from Joe."

Ava felt fear clutch her by the throat and said, "He won't try to hurt me, will he?"

"No," Patrick replied right away, shaking his head vehemently. "He won't be interested in you. I don't think he was following you to your room. I think he was looking for me."

"Are… are you sure?" Ava asked. The boy's reassurances did little to alleviate her concern.

"Pretty sure," he said with confidence.

"Okay," Ava said. "I'll try to help you. My new friend." She squeezed Floppy in a tight hug and smiled at Patrick. The ghostly boy returned the smile.

20

Guests

Mommy was pacing in the cafeteria. Daddy and Ava sat together at the table, watching her. She mumbled to herself, and Ava thought she looked a little like a crazy person.

She leaned over to her father and in a single word voiced her concerns. "Daddy?"

He bent toward her and said, "Mommy's okay, kiddo. She's just a little... nervous, I guess, is the best way to put it. Tonight is a big deal for her, and she wants to make sure everything is perfect."

Ava was a little on edge herself but for a different reason. It had been a handful of days since her encounter with the shadowy form coming down the stairs and then finding Patrick in her room. She hadn't seen the boy again after that. She was worried that maybe Joe had finally gotten him and was taking his revenge. Or maybe the Collector had taken Patrick away and she would never see him again.

She hated both ideas. She had finally made a real friend and to lose him to the Collector, taking him far away, would be a terrible blow. But even worse, she couldn't stand the thought of Patrick being hurt by the ghost of the bully. She tried her best to put all that out of her head for Mommy's special dinner party, but she wasn't having an easy time of it.

She was also without the comfort of Floppy. As usual, she had wanted the stuffed rabbit close at hand but Mommy had other ideas.

"No," she had said with finality. "You're not touting that mangy old thing around in front of Mommy's guests. They'll think I don't take proper care of you, letting you play with a dirty old thing like that. And I have half a mind to agree."

Ava grew deeply concerned that Mommy was on the edge of changing her mind regarding Ava keeping Floppy. If she made the girl throw him away, how would she ever explain it to Patrick? He might be more heartbroken over the loss than herself, though she couldn't imagine anyone caring for anything as much as she loved that rabbit.

So, Floppy sat carefully tucked away in her bed. She saw to it that he was comfortable, and the sheet and blanket were pulled up nice and tight to keep him warm and safe. Still, she couldn't stop herself from wishing desperately that he was cradled in her arms at that very moment.

Daddy gave her a reassuring hug. She smiled up at him.

"Where are they?" Mommy hissed.

"Take it easy, Candace; it's only three minutes after."

"I will not take it easy, *Mike*," she emphasized his name with a hint of acid. Daddy took this in stride, not joining her in her frustration. "This could be the most important night of my career. You understand that, right?"

"I get it," he said, "but can you take the crazy down a notch or two? You're upsetting our daughter."

Mommy's eyes flicked to Ava and the girl recoiled against the chairback. But then the woman's face softened a little. A tide of relief washed upon the little girl's heart.

Mommy expelled a heavy sigh, and her shoulders dropped back down from being hunched up. "Sorry, Baby. I've just been waiting for this break for a very long time, and I don't want anything to go wrong. That makes Mommy a little antsy. Okay?"

Ava offered a weak smile and said, "Okay, Mommy. But you don't have to be nervous. I believe in you." They were words both parents had often spoken to Ava when the girl tried to do something new and struggled.

Daddy grinned at the parroting and said, "Yeah. You got this, Babe."

"Thanks, you guys. I just…"

But Mommy was interrupted by knocking. She gasped and spun around. Three well-dressed people – a man and two women – were visible through the glass door.

Mommy was frozen for about three seconds then exploded into action. She scurried toward the door, nearly tripping over her own feet in the process. She managed to catch herself and hoped the flub wasn't noticeable to her guests. The hint of a crooked smirk that ghosted across the man's lips told her otherwise. But there was nothing to do about it now except to make certain the rest of the evening went smoothly.

She pasted on the world's largest smile as she reached the door and pulled it open for them. "Welcome!" she said – in her judgment a little overenthusiastically. She chided herself to tone it down. *You don't want to drive them off in the first five minutes, do you?* she thought.

One by one, the three guests stepped inside and drank in their surroundings.

The first to enter was an older woman with graying hair. She sported a simple yet elegant black dress. She wore a lot of jewelry. And by the expression on her face, she wasn't impressed. She wrinkled her nose as she sniffed. She said, "It's not exactly the Hilton, is it?"

"Oh, Mary, cut it out," said the next woman, rolling her eyes as she came through the door. She was much younger and her attire significantly more colorful than her predecessor. She wore a neat red business suit and a white blouse with a plunging neckline. She also wore jewelry, but her rule seemed to be 'less is more.' Her manner served as a counterpoint to Mary. She wore an easy smile and glided with grace into the converted cafeteria.

"I don't think I will, Rosy," Mary replied coldly.

"Do give it a rest," the third guest intoned in a deep basso voice. He was tall and lean, his dark skin a contrast to his white suit. He walked in an easy, unhurried manner and displayed a pleasant smile that Ava liked right away.

She had not met any of these people before, though Mommy and Daddy had spoken with each of them at various points over the last year or so. They were interested in Mommy's music and also something to do with the new home they had moved into. Ava didn't understand almost any of it.

"Charles, it's so nice to see you again," Mommy said. Daddy was at her side now, shaking hands and exchanging greetings and pleasantries with the newcomers.

"So, Candance," Charles said stepping forward into the space, but looking directly at Ava, "Are you going to introduce me to this ravishing young lady?"

Ava shrank down in her seat a little but giggled.

"Oh, yes!" Mommy replied, "Where is my head? Charles, Mary, Rosy, this is our daughter Ava."

Charles strolled over to the table and extended a large hand. "Pleased to make your acquaintance," he said, bowing.

Ava giggled again and took his hand, shaking it – she hoped – like a grown-up would.

"Hello, Ava. It's nice to meet you," Rosy said. "How do you like your new home?"

Ava froze. Mommy had drilled into Ava that she was not to speak to the guests unless spoken to. Mommy had also said that she doubted any of them would speak to her. Yet here she was.

"I..." Ava stammered. "It's... it's big, isn't it?"

Rosy laughed. "Yes. It's bigger than my apartment in the city, that's for sure. I'm a little jealous."

Mary made no motion to acknowledge Ava's existence. She merely watched the proceedings with detachment and disinterest. She wrinkled her nose again and made a sniffling sound, but that was about it.

"What's the agenda for this evening, Mike?" Charles asked. "Are you going to give us a tour of your curious facility first?"

Daddy cleared his throat and tossed a glance at his wife. "Actually, I think we'll do dinner first. Then we can give you all the tour and talk shop."

"Oh, good," Rosy interjected. "I'm famished. I haven't eaten anything all day but a power bar and a salad."

"It doesn't show," Mary mumbled. This earned a look of warning from Rosy, who was not plump by any stretch of the imagination as Mary implied.

Mike clapped his hands and grinning said, "Oh, that was a close one! I almost planned power bars and salads for dinner. Instead, I decided on brisket."

Rosy and Charles chuckled. Mary rolled her eyes.

Mommy gave Daddy a look, but he ignored it.

Mike continued, "Everyone has place settings at the table, so go ahead and find your nameplate."

"How chic," Mary said dryly as she headed for the table in unenthusiastic strides.

Everyone found their places and sat. Daddy left to retrieve their dinner from the kitchen. The others distracted themselves right away by falling into casual conversation about things Ava could not comprehend. Ava, however, who was already seated did everything in her power to keep from gasping.

Through the glass of the double doors leading into the hallway, she saw a face staring at them. It was Floppy. They locked eyes and if the stuffed animal could have done so, she believed it would have dropped her a wink. Then he dropped out of sight.

It must be Patrick playing around, she thought. Stuffed animals don't just get up and walk around on their own.

The door creaked slowly open. None of the adults noticed.

Ava went cold when she saw Floppy's head and one of his drooping arms appear around the edge of the door.

She might have been amused save for two things. The first was that Patrick playing around like this during Mommy's big special dinner with people from the record label would not go over well with Mommy… and definitely not the sour old woman in the black dress.

The second was inexplicable, but Ava got the impression that what was happening here was neither silly nor playful. She got the sinking feeling that something dreadful was about to happen.

21

Dinner

Ava watched in frozen fascination as Floppy walked through the door seemingly of his own accord. He only made it two steps before the door quietly clicked closed behind him and he sat on the floor. Her eyes went to the stuffed creature's face and got stuck on its glassy eyes.

They appeared no different than they had since she first found the toy in a room on the upper floor of the old school, yet now looking into them caused a portentous sensation to seize the little girl's chest. And it wasn't a good one. It made the flesh of her back feel crawly and unsettled.

The adult conversation carried on apace around the table as none of them had witnessed the entrance of the stuffed rabbit. At least there was that much. But what was happening? Her new friend, Patrick, seemed to be behind it, whatever it was but she couldn't begin to imagine what he was up to. She didn't get the impression that he was merely goofing around. That didn't fit what she felt. But...

Maybe she was wrong?

Floppy slowly rose to his feet. He didn't stand like a person would, of course. He had no knees to bend and didn't have to shift his body around like everyone she knew. Instead, it was like an invisible hand grabbed him by the back of his neck and lifted him to make him appear like he was standing.

The rabbit unhurriedly raised one leg, thrust that side of his body forward, and brought the leg down. He then lifted the next leg and repeated. He continued this measured progress for two more steps and then dropped back to a sitting position. Floppy gave a little shake of his head, then went still again.

A stray thought lanced through Ava's mind. If Mommy saw Floppy sitting on the floor during her special dinner she might lose it with Ava. She would think Ava left the rabbit there and then the girl would be in a world of trouble.

Her mind raced for solutions. Maybe she could be excused to go to the bathroom, snatch the stuffy, and take it back to her room. If Patrick was still waiting beyond the door, she could tell him to knock it off as now was not a good time for… whatever this was supposed to be.

Floppy slowly turned his head from side to side as if looking around to make sure the coast was clear. Then, he lifted from the floor and took another three steps before dropping back down. He turned his face toward Ava and stared at her. A deeply uncomfortable wave rolled through her, twisting her stomach in knots.

"Eat your dinner, dear," Daddy whispered into her ear.

Ava yelped loudly, startled by the intrusion of her father's voice into the intensifying moment. She whipped her saucer-eyed face around to stare at him.

The conversation around the table went silent and everyone's faces shot to her. As her awareness of what had just transpired dawned on her, her own face started to warm with embarrassment. But it was Mommy's expression that threatened to undo her.

Mommy's glowering visage was at once horrified and laced with restrained rage. Her nostrils flared and her eyes communicated a wordless warning to her young daughter. *Don't you dare screw this up for me*, it said.

She didn't want to. That was the last thing she wanted. Mommy had been on edge for a long time about her music and her plans for the old, abandoned school. Ava wanted Mommy to have everything she dreamed about.

Daddy didn't seem to notice what was going on with Mommy, however. He was fixed on Ava. He said, "Whoa, you okay, kiddo?"

"I... I..." Ava started and fumbled for words as she glanced around the table at all the other faces. They ranged from curious to contempt. Though Ava wouldn't have been able to sort out the finer nuances of these, she caught the gist. She turned back to Daddy and said, "You scared me."

"Scared you?" Daddy asked. "Babe; I only told you to eat your dinner. I've done it a thousand times."

"I was... thinking about something else," Ava said. "Sorry."

Daddy chuckled and tousled his daughter's hair. "That's okay, kiddo. You just surprised us. That's all. No harm done." He turned a pointed look at Mommy and held her gaze for a handful of heartbeats. Though no words passed between them, it was clear to Ava that something was communicated. But that wasn't her concern. She had to take care of Floppy.

Her mouth dropped open to ask if she could go to the bathroom and her body readied to get up from the table. At the same time, she turned to lock her gaze on the wayward rabbit.

But it was gone.

A frigid pit of foreboding formed in her chest. What was Patrick up to now? And how was he doing this?

Ava turned her attention all around in hopes of finding the stuffy. But she couldn't see it anywhere.

That's when she felt a touch of something cloth tapping on her leg.

Her chest started heaving with panicked breaths. Her face flushed with tingly heat and tears threatened to form in her eyes and spill down her cheeks. Her fingernails scratched the surface of the table leaving faint marks.

All the while, the tapping continued.

"Babe, what's wrong?" Daddy said. The conversation around the table had died again, and once more all the attention was focused on her. She was desperate to get it off her as soon as possible but was at a complete loss as to what to do.

Then the earlier inspiration struck again.

"Daddy, I need to go to the bathroom."

Daddy's brow drew down. He was silent for a moment as he mulled this over. It was clear he struggled to believe her stated need was the real problem.

He dipped his head in acknowledgment and said, "Okay, kiddo. Don't take too long, though. And don't forget to wash your hands."

Relief exploded through Ava. At the same time, she reached under the table and snagged the tapping hand of Floppy, stilling its incessant motion. She felt the rabbit go limp.

She pushed away from the table, pulling Floppy up, and hugging him to her chest. She turned away from the table, thinking about having a word with Patrick regarding this little stunt when Mommy cleared her throat noisily. She had made it all of two steps away from the table.

Ava's shoulders tensed, her nose wrinkled, and her lips parted slightly, revealing clenched teeth... but she did not turn around.

"Look at me, little one," Mommy said in a chilly tone.

Ava slowly turned.

"I believe I told you to put that ratty thing away before dinner," she said.

"Yes, Mommy," Ava said, not wanting to rock the boat by arguing. She *had* put Floppy away. She had obeyed.

"Make it your first stop to do so," Mommy said. "I don't want to see him the rest of the night. Understood?"

"Yes, Mommy," Ava repeated.

But before Ava could follow through with the instruction, Floppy lifted his head and began to look around. Then it lifted a hand and pointed in the direction of the table.

None of them made a sound but everyone stared at the stuffed rabbit with varying degrees of astonishment. Perhaps except for Mary who seemed perpetually unimpressed. A slight sneer twitched at one corner of her lips.

"Ava, what...?" Mommy began but ceased when Floppy pushed his way out of the little girl's arms, scurried across the floor on all fours, and leaped onto the table. Everyone at the table gasped and leaned back. None had the presence of mind to vacate their seat, however.

Floppy was hunched forward and cast quick looks around the table. His attention landed on Rosy and stayed on her. With tremendous speed, the stuffed creature lurched forward. Along the way, Floppy reached down and snatched the steak knife up from Rosy's place setting.

As the rabbit approached, instinct kicked in and she attempted to back away, but too late. In the space of a heartbeat, the rabbit finished his journey and rammed the knife into one of Rosy's widening eyes. It went in up to the hilt. She jerked and threw herself back so hard she sent her chair arcing away. She crashed into the ground, her body convulsing, her hands forming into claws. Her mouth worked for a few more seconds in a soundless scream, then she went still.

A stunned moment followed, and everyone stared in horror and disbelief at what had just played out. Then came the sound of four chairs scraping along the floor as those still alive hurriedly pushed away from the table... away from Floppy.

22

Trap

Ava's heart constricted at the horrific sight of the dead woman lying on the floor, still attached to her fallen chair. She forced her focus back to the table, back to Floppy. It was impossible what she saw there.

She didn't think it was Patrick behind this any longer. This had to be the work of the mean boy. Joe. Patrick had been wrong about him. He would hurt the living. He had murdered someone just now.

The stuffed rabbit that had always hung inert in her grip or was crushed in her hugs now stood on top of the table. Its raggedy stuffed countenance she had found so adorable was now a portent of menace. He turned his head this way and that, taking in the people who had fled their places. It appeared as if it might be choosing who to go after next.

Mary, the older grumpier woman wasn't interested in waiting to find out. She made a break for the door leading outside. She didn't move particularly quickly in her black dress.

She arrived at the door and tried the handle. It gave only a little, then resisted her effort. She tried again with the same result. She spun and located Mike. "It's locked," she screamed.

An instant later Charles was at her side. He shoved her out of the way and tried to unlock the door until the strain of the effort showed on his face. He tried twice more but the door was not going to obey. All the while he shot fearful glances at Floppy.

So far, the rabbit seemed content to remain on the table, merely watching them. Ava doubted that would last. A feeling deep in her gut told her more blood was on the way. And soon.

"Mike, how do you get this thing unlocked?" Charles shouted.

Mike had moved toward the set of doors leading to the hallway... the same door through which Floppy had entered the cafeteria space. He maneuvered Ava and Candance behind him.

"I didn't lock it!" he yelped, never tearing his eyes from the fluffy threat atop the table. "But there's a thumb switch."

"It's not working," Charles replied after trying it. He removed his hand and turned his complete attention to the threat.

Floppy seemed focused on perhaps one of the two remaining guests. It was impossible to tell which. His glassy gaze betrayed little. He stooped with deliberate slowness and drew another knife from the table. He let the weapon hang at his side, but it was no less intimidating for it.

Daddy reached behind himself and beyond his family cowering in confusion behind him. His hand came to rest on the door. He felt around blindly until he found the door handle. He turned it and the door popped open without a problem.

"This way," he urgently whispered to Charles and Mary, then ushered Candance and Ava into the hallway. Charles and Mary kept their backs pressed against the wall as they inched along it, keeping their eyes on the murderous stuffed creature as they went.

Once she was in the hallway, Ava broke free and trotted toward her room. She hesitated, however. What if Joe were in there, waiting for her? He was clearly behind this, though she could not fathom why. As she stared at her closed bedroom door, hands fell hard on her shoulders and spun her around. When the world finished twisting, she was met by a crazed set of eyes – her mother's. Mommy was kneeling in front of her like she sometimes did when she wanted to speak carefully to the girl. Now, however, she looked like she was ready to come out of her skin.

"What is happening?" she demanded. "Your rabbit... that thing... it killed...." She couldn't get a hold of a single line of thought and dissolved into sputtering and stammering.

"Hey," Daddy barked at her. "Not now. We gotta move."

The door slammed after Charles and Mary came through. They were now rapidly backing away from the double doors. Ava glanced around Mommy, and through the glass with wire cross-hatching inside. She watched as Floppy finally jumped down from the table. He had been facing the door and presumably was headed in their direction.

"How do we get out of here?" Charles asked. "That thing will be here any second."

"The closest way out is through a window in our room," he said, heading for the first door of the hallway. He tried to open it but the knob wouldn't respond.

"Locked," he said, moving to the next door – the one leading to Ava's room. He tried to open it, but that door was also locked. He grunted and shouted a formless noise at the door.

"It doesn't want us to leave," Mary groaned in despair.

One of the double doors started to push open and Charles lunged. He shoved it back into place with his shoulder. "What about these doors? Do they lock so we can keep it out?"

"No locks on this side," Daddy admitted.

"Then I'll just have to hold them closed until you can find a way out."

Mommy was still on her knees before Ava, though she no longer paid attention to the girl. Instead, she rocked back and forth, mumbling repeatedly, "This isn't happening, this isn't happening, this isn't...."

Daddy was at her side, hauling her to her feet. "Knock it off!" he shouted in her face. "I'm trying to keep us alive here, and I don't need you losing it. Got it?"

She froze solid, her hands clenching and unclenching at her side, fingers splayed, then curling into claws. Her lips peeled away from her teeth in a snarl and her mouth worked but no words came forth.

"Holy mother of mercy!" Charles suddenly intoned in a strained tone as he pressed his hands against the double doors and leaned into them. "I'm having trouble keeping these closed."

Mike rushed to his side and took one of the doors, leaving Charles to focus on the other.

"How can such a little creature be so strong?" Mary spat in disgusted disbelief. "And what *is* that thing?"

"It's just a toy!" Mommy said, surprising them all by forming a coherent sentence.

"Floppy's not doing it," Ava whined. "It's..." she glanced around to see if the ghostly boy was anywhere to be seen. When she saw the hallway contained only living souls, she concluded in a tone of hushed awe, "I think it's Joe."

"Who's Joe?" Daddy demanded, straining to keep his door closed. Floppy was evidently alternating between doors, testing Daddy and Charles one at a time.

"He's a ghost who lives here," she admitted. "Patrick came into my room and told me about him."

"Patrick?" Mommy asked in a quavering voice.

Ava nodded solemnly. "He's the ghost of a little boy that died here a long time ago."

Mary scoffed. "Ridiculous," she said.

"Is that any harder to believe than a killer stuffed rabbit who's almost stronger than I am?" Charles said through gritted teeth. Floppy had switched to his door.

"Baby, what are you talking about?" Mommy asked, her voice full of fear.

Before Ava could answer, the door Charles had been straining to keep closed burst open, sending the man stumbling into the hallway. He barely managed to stop from colliding with Mary. The older woman screeched anyway as she scampered away.

Once Daddy realized the stuffed animal was in the hallway he darted away from it. Floppy swiped at his ankles with the knife but missed. He backpedaled quickly and rejoined Ava and his wife.

"There's another door leading outside at the end of the adjoining hallway," he said. "Come on."

"How do we know that one's not also locked?" Mary protested.

"Fine," Daddy snapped. "You stay here and get butchered while we check."

Mary moaned but then grunted in acquiescence. With the decision made, they moved as a group away from the rabbit and further down the hallway. When they came to the junction, they all glanced down the hallway of the second wing. To their dismay, they all witnessed four menacing disembodied shadows floating in midair blocking their path of egress.

Four? Ava thought as she looked on in disbelief. *Who are the others?* But there was no ready answer.

"Then again, maybe not," Daddy grumbled. They were nearing the stairs, and he chanced a glance in their direction to make sure there wasn't an entity of some kind approaching from that way. When he saw it was clear, he said, "Okay everyone. Looks like up is the only way we can go."

Almost all of them burst into action without further prodding. All except Mary who stood paralyzed at the base of the stairs. Her head turned to face one direction, then the other, soaking in the multitude of threats coming after them.

"Mary, get a move on, *now!*" Charles shouted from halfway up the stairs.

That was enough to get her going. She spun and stumbled up the first few steps. She regained herself but still struggled to take the steps competently thanks to a combination of her over-taxed nerves and high-heeled shoes.

The others had arrived at the top of the first landing and moved on to the next set of steps. Mary's breaths were coming in panicky gasps, and she continued to throw glances over her shoulder toward the base of the steps. There the stuffed creature stood, knife dangling at his side, but not moving to come up the stairs.

When Mary arrived at the landing, she made to follow the others up the next part. However, a figure stood in her way. Ava never saw the figure but if she had she would not have understood.

The ghostly visage of Patrick glowered at the woman with hateful eyes. He raised his arms and clawed his fingers. He growled a threatening roar and lurched at her.

She screamed and jolted backward… but soon there was no floor under her feet. Only stairs. Her arms wheeled uselessly in a cartoonish manner, and she plummeted down gravity's merciless well.

Her neck and back landed hard on the steps. She felt her neck snap and her head shift unnaturally as she tumbled and rolled down the unforgiving slope. She landed in a heap, staring up, unable to move. She stared at the ceiling of the hallway.

Soon, the rabbit slowly slid into her field of vision. She tried to scream but not even her lungs wanted to work. The most she could manage was a slight coughing noise.

Floppy raised the knife over his head and held it there, allowing the sight of it to fill her with utter terror. Suddenly he began to stab the incapacitated woman repeatedly.

23

Studio

"Where's Mary?" Charles asked as they reached the top of the stairs. He whipped his face around to locate the woman but she was nowhere to be found. Then they heard her scream back the way they came. This was followed by the simultaneous sounds of a thud and sickening crack.

Charles turned to descend the stairs again intending to discover what happened to Mary. He made it down two steps but Daddy shot out a hand and snatched a handful of the man's fine silk shirt at his shoulder.

"Stop," he shouted.

Charles turned a threatening expression on Daddy, but he didn't even flinch.

"Too late," he said to Charles. The two simple words appeared to do the trick. Charles dropped a reluctant nod and Daddy let go of his shirt.

"Where to now?" Charles asked, coming up the two steps. Then in a snide growl, he added, "I take it there's no exits up here."

"It's going to be a bit of a drop," Daddy began, "But we can climb out one of the windows."

"I don't like that," Candance said, a look of terror in her eyes.

"Would you prefer staying here with the rabbit or whatever those other things were?" he snapped. Mommy's mouth became a tight line as she recoiled. She also appeared to diminish in size.

Ava screamed as she was the only one not absorbed in the conversation. She had kept her attention fixed on the stairs. If Joe was going to come at them, that would be the place from which he approached.

Sure enough, Floppy lumbered into view around the corner at the landing. He moved slowly like he was dragging himself. Ava felt like this was more for show than anything else. If Joe wanted, she believed he could make the rabbit scurry at them quickly. He was toying with them.

The adults, startled by her scream, turned as one to watch the approaching rabbit. Now its ragged countenance was splashed with blood. It left little red streaks on the floor as it moved.

"Move!" Charles boomed.

Daddy grabbed Ava and hauled her away. Mommy was right by their side.

Ava's face was buried in her Daddy's shoulder as he ran but she peeked up and watched as Charles brought up the rear, casting occasional glances behind him. But then the man did something she didn't expect. He slowed, halted, and started to turn.

They reached the door to Mommy's studio. It had been propped open in anticipation of the tour and demonstration they had planned to give to Mommy's music people. Daddy set Ava down and guided her into the room while he remained at the door.

Mommy came next and Daddy made sure she entered, then he turned his face, expecting Charles. But the man wasn't there. He was still halfway down the hall.

"Charles, this way!" Daddy shouted. From inside the studio, Ava beheld her father with deep worry. What if he stayed out in the hallway to wait for the other man and Joe made something bad happen out there? Daddy took a tentative step away from the door and back into the hallway causing Ava's heart to leap.

She surged toward the door, but Mommy was right there to stop her. She wrapped her arms around her daughter, preventing her from running anywhere. "No," Mommy shrieked as she held her daughter fast.

Daddy turned his head to see what the fuss was about and when he determined all was still relatively well with his family he returned his attention to the hallway. To Charles.

The older black man stood like a guardian statue facing away.

"Charles, what are you doing? Get in here!"

Charles gave a single shake of his head and replied, "No, sir. Not this old Marine. I have never turned aside from a threat, and I will not run from some child's stuffed toy, no matter the menace. I will stand my ground and fight to give you all a chance to escape. Even if this is my last stand. *Semper Fidelis*, sir."

Daddy was now several paces away from the door. He was about to argue the point when he witnessed the head of Ava's stuffed rabbit crest at the top of the stairs.

"Good luck," Daddy said.

Charles shifted his position slightly so that he now held a fighting stance. He gave another small shake of his head. "I'm a marine. We don't traffic in luck."

Mike nodded then darted for the studio door. Once inside he slammed it shut and locked it.

"Where's Charles?" Mommy asked in a voice that seemed about to shatter like glass.

"He's giving us a chance," her husband replied. "Help me get this soundproof panel off this window."

Daddy rushed to the window and began to work at removing a big slab of wood painted black with gray sound-dampening foam attached. Mommy spared the door a forlorn glance then rushed to the other side of the window. It was no easy chore to pry the wood away.

Ava watched them for a few seconds then turned back to the door. She was so used to carrying Floppy with her everywhere she went that she felt naked without him. At the same time, she wanted little to do with the rabbit after what she had witnessed the stuffed creature do at the dinner table.

No, she thought. *That isn't Floppy's fault. It's the mean boy. It's Joe.*

Muffled noises filtered through from the other side of the door. It sounded like shouting, then thumping. More shouting and thudding noises followed.

Ava took a step toward the door.

"No!" Mommy shrieked. "Ava, stay away from the door!"

Ava jumped at the sound of her mother's screeched command. She hugged her arms around her middle as she glanced at Mommy. The woman wore an unnerving expression Ava had never seen on her before. She was wild-eyed and her cheeks appeared sunken like a starvation victim. Her skin was pale and she trembled.

A loud bang resounded through the studio as something collided powerfully with the closed steel door. The rectangular window which would have revealed what was happening outside had been permanently covered with a smaller wooden panel and the whole back of the door was covered in sound-dampening foam anyway. But it didn't keep all of the sound out.

A muffled scream slipped through. It was louder than almost all of the previous sounds Ava had heard come through the door since entering the studio. All of them except the banging on the door a moment earlier.

"Come on, we almost got it," Daddy urged in a strained voice. Ava whipped around in time to see her parents easing the big panel away from the window. Daddy swung around to Mommy's side of the window, and they unceremoniously dumped the panel. It tottered and fell onto some sound equipment which made Mommy wince.

In the next moment, Daddy was right back at the window, working to get it open. There came a click and Daddy pushed the window open. It tilted from the bottom outward and the top slanted into the room. The opening looked large enough for each of them to slip through one at a time.

"That's a long drop," Mommy muttered. "How are we going to keep from breaking our necks?"

Daddy scoured the room, then said, "Maybe we can use a mic cord or something?"

There came another click, this one from across the room. The door had unlocked seemingly of its own accord and the steel behemoth creaked slowly and noisily open.

Through the doorway, they could see the bottom of Charles's legs. The rest of him lay in the hall beyond the door so they could not see him. Blood pooled beneath him.

Standing framed by the doorway was the ragged and blood-splattered countenance of Floppy. He held a knife that dripped red.

24

Window

"Ava," Mommy hissed as she bent forward and beckoned with both hands to her daughter. "Get back."

Ava was too transfixed on Floppy to see her mother's urgent gestures, but she heard the woman's call. She took a few slow, measured steps backward.

The stuffed monstrosity tracked her every move but remained standing in the doorway.

When Ava reached her mother, the woman grabbed her and guided her around so that she stood behind Mommy.

Daddy reached for a microphone, cautiously removed it from its stand, and started gathering up the black cord. He was already problem-solving how he was going to use the cord to escape. He'd tie one end off to something stationary and use the cord to lower his family out the window. The problem was that he had never been a Boy Scout and thus possessed no merit badges regarding tying knots.

He followed its snaking path to where it was plugged into the system. He quickly crouched and unplugged it. He shot right back up and started inching toward the window. He did his best to keep an eye on the rabbit but there was so much equipment to navigate around that he had to occasionally look away.

Not that the rabbit seemed at all interested in him. The thing seemed to be focused on Ava. He vowed to himself that if the creature suddenly went after her, it would have to deal with him first.

He reached the window after what felt like forever and turned to tie one end around the place where the window tilted on an axis to open. He loathed taking his focus off the murderous stuffed animal, but this was perhaps their only hope of escape. He just had to leave the observation of their enemy to his wife, which was something else he didn't exactly feel comfortable with. She had been fraying at the edges for days over tonight and now that the evening had gone completely sideways, the woman appeared to be losing her hold on reality.

When he'd done the best that he could, he whipped around to face the doorway once more. He was half-surprised to find the rabbit hadn't moved but was happy to accept the fact.

It was as if the rabbit were waiting for everyone to give their full attention. It casually tossed the knife aside. The weapon clattered on the floor not far away. Then Floppy executed a deep, theatrical bow.

It paused like it was waiting for something. Applause maybe?

The human inhabitants of the room stood motionless, each of them certain the next terrible thing was only a heartbeat or two away. But nothing happened. The stuffed creature stayed as it was.

Daddy motioned for his wife and daughter to come over to him. However, the instant Mommy nodded, Floppy's head shot up to stare at them. He turned his face from Mommy to Daddy, then finally landed on Ava. Ava sucked in a startled gasp. With incredible strength and speed, the rabbit leaped and landed on the floor amid the family with Mommy and Ava on one side and Daddy on the other. Everyone scurried back from the minuscule figure that had wreaked so much havoc in such little time.

The toy rabbit turned his face from Daddy to Mommy and Ava. He watched the girls for a while, then slowly turned his face to Daddy. It took a slow step in his direction.

"Stop it!" Ava shouted at Floppy's back.

Floppy halted, then turned his head slightly, indicating it had noticed.

"You leave my Daddy alone, Joe!"

With a hop, Floppy turned completely around to behold the girl. Mommy yelped and hugged her daughter tighter.

"Hush, Baby," Mommy whispered into her daughter's ear. Ava felt her mother tremble uncontrollably.

Floppy tilted his head to one side as he considered something.

No, Ava reminded herself. *Not Floppy*. Floppy was only cloth and stuffing shaped like a rabbit. Joe was controlling it.

"Go away, mean boy," Ava continued, ignoring her mother. "Go away forever and leave us alone."

Floppy's head came up from its tilt... then started slowly descending to the opposite side in another tilt to mirror the first.

When his head reached the shoulder it stopped, hesitated, then started to rise and arc back the way it came... but a little faster.

Soon Floppy's head was tilting the other way again and rising back to go the other way. It was moving a little faster yet. It reached the opposite shoulder again and immediately started journeying to the other side once more. Faster. When it reached that shoulder, it picked up speed and was soon hitting the shoulder on the other side. Now the head was rocking back and forth at a good clip.

It continued doing so, going faster and faster until the head was practically a blur.

Without warning, the rabbit's head stopped rocking, stood straight up, and the stuffed animal leaped high into the air. Their eyes worriedly traced its path.

The rabbit landed in a heap on the floor. It showed no signs of movement.

Silence fell upon the room. No one even wanted to breathe for fear of the palpable nature of the tension.

No one even dared move for an eternity.

Mommy was the first to broach the quiet stillness.

"Is... is it over?" she asked. There was such hope in her words, though her voice was strained and cracking. Ava wanted to turn around and hug her mother, to comfort her.

But she didn't feel like it was over.

Daddy grunted and both Mommy and Ava shot their attention to him. The man still held the microphone in his hand as he darted forward. With his free hand, he seized Floppy, then turned and flung the thing out the window as hard as he could. Ava watched as the rabbit sailed into the darkness and was swallowed up by it.

He stood in front of the window, breathing raggedly as he bared gritted teeth that way, gazing out into the night. His shoulders heaved and he grunted another angry noise.

He turned to Ava and said, "Sorry kiddo, but we're just going to have to get you a new stuffy."

"But Daddy, it wasn't Floppy doing the bad things. It was Joe."

"Still," Daddy said, "I don't think..." but he never got the chance to finish. He yelped in surprise as the microphone was yanked out of his hand by an unseen force. "What in the...?"

That was the last thing Ava ever heard her Daddy say.

The microphone had jerked away from him but now flew back at him. It moved like a living thing.

In an instant, the cord had wrapped itself around his neck and squeezed. His jaw dropped open, and his mouth worked but no more words came out. There were only the truncated noises of his failed attempts to breathe.

"Daddy!" Ava screamed.

Her mother shouted her husband's name and reached out a helpless hand toward him.

Ava's Daddy staggered and struggled, shooting both hands up the undo the cord choking him but to no avail. He found himself in front of the window, eyes bulging, elbows thrashing as he attempted to dislodge the cord. Then it was as if he was struck by an invisible wrecking ball.

He was suddenly lifted off his feet and thrown through the partially open window. Glass shattered and the glistening shards tumbled through the night as he passed through the window. He was momentarily suspended in the air outside the old school having reached the apex of his swing outward. Then gravity took over and he dropped. The microphone cord was still secured on the window frame and went taut when he reached the end of his downward journey.

His neck snapped and his arms went limp, dangling at his side as his body bounced against the brick edifice.

Above his dying form, his girls screamed with grief and terror.

25

WEB

With the terror unseen, Mommy quickly took hold of her daughter's hand and turned to run. They didn't make it very far.

A rack console on castor wheels rolled abruptly into their path. Across the room, a sound mixer powered up by itself and began sparking. Mommy maneuvered Ava around the wheeled cart.

The cart slid into their path again, rumbling along the floor.

Mommy screamed at it as she pulled Ava toward herself, cradling her in her arms.

"Leave us alone! Haven't you done enough?"

A monitor hummed to life and loud bass noises started thumping from it. Five seconds later the sound was nearly unbearable and both Mommy and Ava covered their ears with their hands. The cacophonous torture was short-lived, however, as the monitor became overloaded and the ring-shaped speaker housed in the black angular box cracked, sparked, and went dead.

"Just stop it!" Mommy screamed.

Distorted and deep laughter tumbled from amplifiers all over the room. The keyboard powered up and random keys danced up and down, sending tumultuous and jarring noise everywhere in the room. Mommy briefly hoped the neighbors had heard the disturbance and called the police to check it out. She didn't know what possible help the police might be in this situation. But they might at least be able to extract her and Ava. Assuming they lived long enough.

At the rate people were dying off, she guessed neither of them had much longer. The thought caused a despairing moan to escape her.

But she wasn't ready to give up yet.

She moved Ava out of the way and lurched toward the rolling cart. She kicked at it with all her might, absently grateful somewhere in the back of her mind that she had chosen to wear flats instead of high heels. The kick landed with ferocious force, fueled by untold centuries of built-up mama bear instinct.

The cart spun away, tottered, and fell over. She was surprised that her gambit had worked and that the path was now clear. They just had to make a break for it.

Mommy jerked Ava forward. The girl cried out at the sudden pressure on her shoulder along with the surprise of being thrust forward. She found herself nearly sprawling ahead but Mommy held her hand steadfastly and balanced her once more. They were running for the open door.

Without warning, something wrapped around her ankle and pulled her foot out from under her. In the next moment, she was horizontal in the air and falling fast, face-first toward the floor. She opened her mouth but didn't even have time to scream. Her belly and chest hit the floor first, but the real pain came a fraction of a second later when her face smacked against the unforgiving tile.

Blood gushed briefly from the woman's nose and sharp pain lanced through her face, radiating downward into her neck, chest, and abdomen. A tingling haze clouded her awareness, and her world was composed only of blackness and stars. Reality quickly reasserted itself and she realized she no longer held her daughter's hand.

Her face jerked here and there until she saw Ava standing a few feet away. The girl's fingers were picking at her grimacing lower lip. Her eyes were squinted, and tears poured down her cheeks. She looked so alone and vulnerable.

Mommy tried to push herself up to standing once more but whatever had pulled her off her feet in the first place still had control of matters. She was dragged across the smooth, cool tile floor, making little streaking sounds as she went. She clawed uselessly at the floor, hoping to halt her regress.

A rumbling from the ceiling started and she glanced up. The drop-ceiling panels were dancing in their metal frame housings. Dust dropped in streamers from the ceiling and some of the tiles cracked. One exploded, sending fibrous tile detritus flying everywhere. Another broke in two sections and they dropped to the floor. Another one split into five pieces and all crumbled apart and dropped.

In the uncovered sections of the ceiling concealed behind the tiles, wires and steel conduit danced and dislodged from brackets holding them in place. The conduit split and tore away from the wiring beneath and then the wiring itself came loose and dangled down into the room.

Now wires and cords hung down like vines in a jungle, swaying and jumping on their own. Power cords tore away from equipment and lashed in what at first appeared like a haphazard fashion. Then the pattern emerged. The wiring lashed and snaked against the wall at varying angles, forming something like a child's drawing of a giant spider's web. It covered the entire wall through which they had intended to escape. Sparks spit forth from the exposed wires all over the web.

She turned her desperate face toward Ava and shouted, "RUN!"

The cord that was wrapped around her ankle lifted her and flung her toward the web shape. She screamed as she approached the sparking structure.

Lights flickered in the studio as Ava whimpered and backed toward the door. She was almost too terrified to move, but mostly she didn't want to abandon her Mommy.

Mommy was thrown against the web, dangled upside-down by the cord attached to her ankle. Bits of wire and plastic coating wrapped around her wrists and legs to hold her in place on the web. She writhed as little live, exposed wires pressed up against her flesh and burned her.

She stared at her daughter and again screamed "Ruuuu..." but then electricity was arcing through and over her body, electrocuting her. Her form writhed and convulsed on the web.

Ava screamed at the top of her lungs as she watched Mommy fry.

Mommy went still and no longer shouted. The room went completely dark, as did the hallway beyond the door.

Ava was truly alone now.

Except for the ghosts.

She turned and obeyed her Mommy's final command. She ran.

Bursting through the door and into the benighted hallway, she was certain something was going to reach out for her and snatch her at any second. Then that would be it. She'd end up like everyone else: Dead.

Nothing did. Instead, she almost tripped over Charles's legs. She turned away from him quickly, not wanting to see even in shadow what had become of him. She had witnessed too much horror as it was. Ava thought seeing one more dead person would be too much. She'd just fall over right then and there, and the evil spirit of Joe would get her and make her dead, too.

Maybe then she'd also be a ghost in this awful place and never able to leave, like Patrick and Joe.

The twisted and sinister laughter poured from the studio behind her echoing unnaturally. She tried her best to cover her ears and block it out. But that was tricky to do when she was trying to run at the same time.

She came to the stairs and started bouncing down them, not worried about moving too fast but she did remove her hands from her ears so she could make use of the rail. The laughter continued behind her, booming – yet it also sounded farther away.

She didn't devote much attention to that, though. She was too focused on just getting out.

But how was she going to do that?

Even though the front door was locked, she might be able to break through the glass. There was a lot of glass, and she didn't think it would be very hard to get through.

She came to the landing and froze momentarily when she saw Mary's body lying in a twisted heap and a pool of blood at the bottom of the stairs. Everything was much darker than when she had come through the first time, but she could see well enough in the moonlight filtering through the high windows lining the hallway.

Her attention darted to her left and the four floating shadows remained where she had last seen them. They did not move or encroach. One of them, however, issues a growing sound... like a dog. It was smaller than the other ones. She even thought she witnessed a hint of canine features in the shorter shadow.

She kept her eyes mostly on the unmoving specters but occasionally cast glances at the motionless woman to make certain she didn't trip over her.

She cringed as she descended the remaining stairs and gave a wide berth to the dead woman. But once she was past her and headed toward the cafeteria and main entrance, she never looked back. She bolted.

She went through the double doors into the cafeteria and glanced toward the door leading outside. She couldn't help but notice Rosy lying dead, soaking in her blood on the floor, still essentially seated, but lying down. She turned away quickly and scurried to the door. She reached a hand forward and rested it on the glass. She had correctly recalled that there was a lot of the fragile material but the doors were comprised of small squares of glass housed in thin wooden cross frames. It would be harder to break than she estimated.

A thought occurred to her. She dropped her hand to the door handle and tried it. It worked without a problem. It wasn't even locked.

She pushed the door open and rushed outside. She darted ahead and made it several steps before freezing. Sitting directly in her path on the walkway was Floppy. His legs were splayed forward, and his body leaned that way as well. Both ears drooped down and he showed no sign of life.

Of course not, Ava thought. Floppy hadn't done anything. It was that mean boy ghost who was trapped in the school. But still…

She cautiously approached the rabbit. She stopped a pace or two away and just stared at him with trepidation. She reached a foot forward and nudged him. Nothing happened. She did it again, but there was still no response.

She was alone. So alone with no family and no friends. She needed a friend. And he had been good for her for a while. Besides, she surmised he was no longer under Joe's power. He was probably too far away from the school.

Ava shot out both her hands, picked him up, tucked him under one of her arms, and continued to run.

It then dawned on her that she had nowhere to go. She had no home as well as no family. She needed help.

That's when she heard the faint tinkling of a bell. She froze, her back going rigid. She slowly turned and stared to her right. She witnessed a lone figure slowly walking down the street. He was tall and dressed in a flowing black robe. A voluminous hood was drawn up so that his face was swallowed in a deep black void.

It was The Collector Patrick had told her about. He was coming her way.

Am I dead, too? She wondered. She shook her head with immediate realization. No, she thought. I'm not.

That's when she witnessed a small congregation of dimly glowing white forms appear near the base of the old school's brick wall. They moved toward the figure. Her breath caught in her throat as she recognized the hazy features of her parents and their three guests. They were spectral, ghostly.

Her face flashed hot with instant grief. Tears streaked her cheeks as she lifted a hand toward them and cried out, "Mommy! Daddy!" The ghostly forms gave no indication they heard her.

The Collector continued to ring his bell until he met the floating apparitions in the street. They huddled for a few seconds, then there was a flash of light. Then they were gone.

But something else took their place.

A pair of headlights appeared at the end of the street. She thought about it for a second and then, still sobbing, ran toward them. She didn't stop until she was almost in the middle of the road. She raised her unoccupied hand in the air and waved it back and forth to get the driver's attention. He showed no sign of stopping.

She realized too late that standing in the street was probably a dangerous idea. She'd never crossed a street alone as Mommy and Daddy had always insisted one of them stay with her.

The oncoming car screeched to a sudden halt and the driver laid on the horn. A man in his late twenties stepped out of the driver's side door and in an angry voice began to berate her.

"Little girl! What's the matter with you? I almost ran you..." but he trailed off as he took in the sight of her. She was disheveled and streaked with blood. He muttered a curse and came around the door to get a better look at her.

He knelt before her. He smelled funny to her like he'd been smoking. But it also didn't smell like the cigarettes Daddy used to smoke. This smell was more... sour than that. More pungent.

"Kid, what happened?"

The barrier broke and she collapsed to her knees sobbing. "They're dead. They're all dead." Those were the only words she could manage between gouts of wracked crying.

"Where?" he asked. She lifted a hand and pointed at the school. He turned, saw the structure, and stiffened. His eyes widened in surprise as he swept his gaze around once more to her. In an awed tone, he asked, "What were you doing in there?"

But she could no longer speak. The grief and terror and everything else that characterized her night overwhelmed her.

He reached into his pocket, extracted his phone, and dialed 911. After a brief conversation with the dispatcher on the line (one in which he refused to divulge his identity) he hung up and knelt before Ava again.

"Help is on the way, Kid," he said. "But I can't hang out. I've got too much stuff in my system and can spare no more points on my license. So, like, do me a favor and forget what I look like, okay?"

He hesitated, carefully picked her up (to which she did not protest), and carried her to the curb on the other side of the street. There was a line of bushes there that Ava eyed suspiciously.

"Sorry to have to cut and run, but the police will be here soon, okay?"

The only response that came from Ava was more sniffles and crying. She hugged the stuffed rabbit tightly to herself as she had done countless times ever since she had found him. The driver gave her a final look, then hurried back to his car, got in, and drove away.

Once he was gone, she found herself staring at the old school across the street. She felt like it was looking at her. Looking and grinning. Grinning like a cat that looks at a bird outside the window that it would like to eat.

She slipped inside the bushes and hid, glancing through them at the school. Hoping it couldn't somehow reach out and get her. There she stayed until the police found her a while later.

School Closes Indefinitely

The following is a selection of an article from the Cedar Park Herald, a local newspaper. Dated April 21, 1987

Following the turbulent events surrounding the suspicious deaths of two students, Cedar Park – the local public school facility of this small town – has been closed perhaps for the final time.

Public Opinion varies on whether this is the correct decision. Dissenters indicate the relative newness of the school and the increased taxes to fund its construction not long ago. Those favoring the school closing cite the emotional damage done to the community. One resident even went so far as to suggest the school might be cursed.

Authorities continue the investigation but an undisclosed inside source indicates perplexity abounds regarding the case. The anonymous source stated, "Every time a new lead crops up they follow it only to run into an abrupt dead end."

Moreover, neighbors living near the school recently reported odd nighttime occurrences, including classroom lights that turn on and off in the middle of the night and suspicious noises from the building. The police have been called to the scene for several such occurrences but no culprits have yet been caught.

For the time being, the previous school facility will be reopened in an emergency measure to finish out the school year. It remains to be seen if Cedar Park School will permanently return to the facility for its public education needs.

Epilogue

Detective Byrd ambled down the hall of the police station, lost in thought. She shook her head but couldn't seem to clear it. The girl's story was, of course, unbelievable. That wasn't what made it so extraordinary, however. The mysterious events surrounding the death of her parents along with three other adults were quite a lot and would take much time and effort to unravel.

No, the thing that was bothering Detective Byrd was one particular part of the story she told – the part that had nothing to do with her or her family. It was the part that featured the history of the school her family had recently bought. Some of the details surrounding the reasons for closing the school were strikingly close to reality, including a handful of facts that had been closely guarded secrets to protect the families of some people who had been involved.

On the other hand, there were elements of the girl's retelling of that story which were far wide of the mark. Byrd considered that perhaps that was to be expected. Ava was only six. How could she be expected to keep that much information straight... especially concerning events that had transpired decades before she had been born?

But still, some of the details the girl had shared were not just wrong. They were way wrong. And it wasn't sitting well with the detective. Something was amiss in a way she could not put her finger on. It was almost as if the girl had received her information from an eyewitness source… but that source had chosen to blatantly lie to the girl about certain things to make it appear as though the guilty were innocent, and the innocent were guilty.

She shook her head again.

She had gone to check with her chief who had been around during the original tragedies to see how he recalled matters. When he asked why she was so interested, she told him everything. The man was just as perplexed as she was.

After that, she decided to clear her head for another few minutes and grab some coffee from the breakroom. The cup was half empty by the time she returned to the room where Ava sat, accompanied by a social worker, where they had been asking her questions.

Ava had been cleaned up, but she would not let go of that ratty old stuffed rabbit. Whenever Detective Byrd looked at the thing, she got a bad feeling.

"Okay, Ava," Byrd said. "Are you ready to talk about what happens next?"

Ava nodded but said nothing. After her story had been told she hadn't been very talkative. Mostly her answers were of the 'yes' or 'no' variety.

"Very good, sweetheart. We're going to spend the next few days looking for relatives of yours. Grandmas, grandpas, aunts, uncles, that sort of thing. It's best if you go to be with one of them. In the meantime, you're going to stay with Ms. Charlotte who's been hanging out with you here for a while. Does that sound okay?"

Ava gave a solemn, absentminded nod. She wasn't making eye contact anymore. Instead, the girl turned her face away and stared off into the distance. Byrd sighed inwardly, feeling a pang of sorrow for the girl. She had been through so much terrible violence that no one should ever have to endure, let alone a six-year-old girl.

But at least the worst of it was over.

***

"Ms. Charlotte?" Ava said as they crossed the parking lot toward the woman's car.

"You can just call me 'Charlotte,' dear. Okay?"

"Okay. Charlotte? Do you live in a nice house with a family?"

Charlotte chuckled. "I live in an apartment complex with my husband, Sweety. And a cat. You're not allergic to cats, are you?"

"No, ma'am," Ava replied. She even seemed to perk up at the mention of the cat. Charlotte was relieved to bring a little happiness to the girl, even if it would be short-lived. The poor thing couldn't stay with her forever. Not if she had blood relatives who could care for her.

Charlotte opened the door to the back seat of her sedan and allowed Ava to crawl up into the seat herself. She didn't have a kid's car seat, but her place wasn't far, so she didn't worry about it. She buckled Ava's seatbelt for her. Once the girl was secure, she closed the back door and got into the driver's seat. She inserted the key into the ignition and started it up.

Charlotte glanced at Ava in the rearview mirror and with a smile, said, "Why do you ask, Ava?"

"I'm not asking," Ava said. "Patrick is."

"Oh! Is that your bunny rabbit's name?"

Ava turned and looked at the empty seat beside her. She stared that way and smiled conspiratorially for a brief moment. Which Charlotte thought was odd.

Ava looked back at the woman and said, "Yup!"

Ava didn't like lying. But she was happy that her friend had been wrong about not being able to leave the school. It turned out that he was tied to the rabbit all along.

And it made her happy that she could bring her friend with her wherever she went.

He seemed pretty happy about it too. As she glanced at him seated beside her in the back seat of Charlotte's car, he was smiling. Though she had to admit, the smile unsettled her a little.

Trial Conclusion

The following is a selection of an article from the Cedar Park Herald, a local newspaper. Dated July 24, 1987

In a bizarre conclusion to an already perplexing situation, the murder trial of Reginald Harris, the former janitor for Cedar Park School, has concluded. He has been rendered criminally insane and will be remanded to a state institution indefinitely.

The defendant made several wild claims during his trial. One of the more disturbing assertions was that he was acting at the behest of his deceased child. He alleges that his son, Patrick Harris, who was found dead earlier this year in a supply closet at the now-closed school, incited the janitor to murder another Cedar Park student – Joseph Henderson – for which Reginald Harris was standing trial. He claimed ghostly visitations with his deceased child and late-night planning sessions regarding how he would perpetrate his malicious crimes.

Mr. Harris maintained that Joseph Henderson and a handful of his classmates were responsible for the death of Patrick Harris. He painted a picture of extended harassment and abuse on the part of Henderson and his companions against Patrick. He alleged his son was a helpless and vulnerable victim. However, internal school records revealed a different picture.

The prosecution made significant use of the fact that Patrick appears to have been a disturbed child and a troublemaker. Several teachers testified to his difficult nature and proclivity to violent outbursts, despite his young age and small stature. The intimation was that the Harris household was unstable. These discrepancies apparently contributed to the judge's legal decision.

Mr. Harris had sole custody of a daughter as well. As of this writing, there is no decision regarding what will become of Maggie Harris. One can only pray she will endure these dark days and not carry them forever as she grows.

The girl's mother could not be reached for comment.